A MONSTROUS VISION . . .

"My art," said the doctor, holding up the scale models, "is the removal of unwanted characteristics and predilections from the cell nucleus and the splicing in of the desirable alternatives. We can target and modify genes for height, weight, heart disorder, precancerous growth. And of course, my own personal signature—red hair and green eyes."

"You can take a cell from a pregnant woman, redesign it, put it back in, and her child will come out whatever way you want?"

"Yes."

"Without her even knowing?"

"Without her knowing."

"My God," Pat gasped, thinking about the staggering implications of his work.

"And you've done it?" she asked, terrified.

The doctor said nothing . . .

Christmas Babies

Christopher Keane
and
William D. Black, M.D.

POCKET STAR BOOKS

New York   London   Toronto   Sydney   Tokyo   Singapore

A Pocket Star Book published by
POCKET BOOKS, a division of Simon & Schuster Inc.
1230 Avenue of the Americas, New York, NY 10020

ISBN: 0-671-72421-5

First Pocket Books printing December 1991

10 9 8 7 6 5 4 3 2 1

POCKET STAR BOOKS and colophon are registered
trademarks of Simon & Schuster Inc.

Cover art by Lisa Falkenstern

Printed in the U.S.A.

TO SUSAN CRAWFORD

Acknowledgments

The authors would like to thank the following for their invaluable contributions: Lorne Crawford, Ann Goldstone, William Martin, Sally Peters, Donna Ryan

PROLOGUE

Fall Springs, Indiana

DAVID MORRIS PRESSED THE SCALPEL INTO THE WOMAN'S flesh and drew it across her abdomen. She was small, barely five feet, and weighed a hundred pounds. It was hard to believe that there was an infant inside Mary Wills's childlike body.

David had been her doctor for several years now and kept a special eye on her throughout her pregnancy. Because she was so young, just twenty, and had a history of illness, David had insisted on weekly checkups and classes in prenatal care. Mary followed his instructions, and he had been confident that the delivery would go without a hitch.

Both patient and doctor had been surprised when Mary went into advanced labor eight weeks early. David worried about the cesarean, an occasionally risky operation, especially when the procedure was unexpected, but there was no way this baby could be delivered normally.

David made the incision, and his assistant used the electrocautery to coagulate the small blood vessels, then a Richardson retractor for exposure. David worked quickly, separating the fascia from the muscles to make room for the baby's delivery. Sweat accumulated beneath his mask, he tried to will his fingers to relax. This was his third night in a row at the hospital, and his stamina was at its limit.

He pushed the patient's bladder away from the uterus and made a transverse incision through the muscle wall, rupturing the membrane. Fluid gushed out, soaking everything and everyone around the operating table. He slid his hand into the uterus to guide the baby. He looked at Mary; her eyes were huge and glazed over. She gave him a weak smile.

The child was pathetically small, with wisps of reddish hair and dull green eyes. When David finally succeeded in squeezing it out, he felt right away that the baby might not live. Its heart was barely beating, its color bad, and sores and lumps covered its skin. He handed the baby to the nurse, who carried it to the infant resuscitator.

Mary's face was white against the sheet, her breathing labored; she was losing blood. David mentally recapped her medical history. Had she been too weak to endure a pregnancy? Should he have discouraged it? She had wanted the child desperately, and together they had done everything to make sure the birth would go smoothly. She had gained enough weight and was, she told him, stronger and happier than she had ever been. Now all their months of work seemed futile.

Her eyes were closed now, and a dry sound escaped from her lips. She was trying to speak. He motioned for his assistant to tend to the closing as he took her hand. She opened her eyes and again tried to speak.

"Don't try to say anything," David told her. "Just lie back and let us do the work."

Instead, she tensed her neck muscles and raised her head an inch or so, looking down along her body, searching for her child. He glanced at the nurse, who was now standing in the doorway, holding the baby in her arms. David could tell by the nurse's expression that the baby was gone.

David looked down at Mary and watched the fact of her child's death register as her eyes clouded over and dimmed. How could she have known?

"Come on, Mary," he said, pressing her hand. "Don't you give up on me; everything's going to be fine."

Her head dropped to the sheet, turning toward him. He felt the muscles in her hand relax; then the tension in her body seemed to flow away. A gurgle rose from her throat as she struggled to speak. "Thank you, Doctor." The barely audible words were her last.

David clenched the sides of the operating table and felt the last of his strength draining out. He stared at the young face on the bloody table. He saw his partner, Ben Brost, take the tiny infant from the nurse and carry it off to Autopsy, cradling it as if it were his own child.

The nurse stuck her head into the operating room and looked at David, his face tense, concerned. "Doctor," she said, "you need some rest." David shook his head. "I have to tell her husband first." Tell her husband what? he wondered. Would he say that green-eyed, red-haired babies were being born every day and that his practice was fast becoming a freak show?

David knew he was never going to reach the reception area. It was too far away, and the hallway was too blurry, nebulous. . . . He tried to put his hands out in front of him to block the floor swelling up at him.

He woke up a few minutes later in his office, on his back, on the faded leather couch. "Hello, Doctor," Ben said, reaching for his pulse.

"I blanked?" David asked.

"Right out."

David tried to stand but found that he was still too dizzy, and he fell back into the cushions.

"Will you take it easy, for chrissake?" Ben said to him, aggravated. "You've had a tough week."

"More like a tough month," David said. "What in the *hell* has been going on around here?"

"Hey, think about it. In twelve years of practice this is your first major problem. There's a miracle for you. We've had a run of bad luck, but it hits everybody sooner or later. At least that's what they told me at medical school."

"Bad luck?" David said, his voice listless. "Two deformed infants, a miscarriage, three failed cesareans, and a mother's death—in three weeks. Bad luck? Add to that three premature deliveries that just barely made it."

Ben nodded. "It's the worst part of being a doctor, dealing with the things you can't control."

4

David relaxed for the first time that night. He wanted to believe what his partner was saying. Ben had a lot of wisdom for a man so young.

David desperately wanted to feel that he was not responsible, that it had been fate or coincidence, that a power greater than his own had decreed that these children were not meant to live. Then he remembered Mary's broken voice saying, "Thank you, Doctor."

Thank you, Doctor? For what? he thought. This was not just fate working here. He had been around operating rooms too long to believe that.

1

Indian Rocks Beach, Florida

THE PHONE RANG, AND PAT HELLER ROLLED OVER TO face the jangling noise. The clock read 2:30 A.M. She grunted and turned back to her sleeping husband.

"Josh!" she said angrily. "Josh!" He wasn't moving. She snatched up the phone and barked, "Hello!" She knew who it was.

"Pat, this is Julie Palmer at the hospital. Sorry to bother you. Is Dr. Heller there?"

"Where else would he be?"

"I have Dr. Ellison here for him."

"A medical tag team. What a thrill."

There was silence on the other end. She knew she had been difficult with the hospital staff over the past few weeks, but there had been too many late-night emergencies. Birth complications. Josh's specialty. "Just a minute," she said, "I'll get him."

She turned back to her husband, who was hanging

over the side of the bed like a dead man. Josh could sleep through anything. His light brown hair fell over his forehead and into his eyes. He was handsome in a ruffled sort of way, and he looked younger than his forty-four years. His mouth drooped open in the middle of a tiny snore.

"Josh." She shook his shoulder. "It's Jim Ellison, at the hospital. Another problem."

"Tell 'em I'm out of town."

"Come on, dear. Time to rise and shine."

He grunted and pulled the covers over his head.

"Josh!"

Suddenly an arm shot out of the blankets, fingers stretching out the tension. Pat placed the receiver in his palm.

"Yeah, Jim," he mumbled, "this is my aura you're talking to here, not me. What's up?"

"You've got to get over here, Josh. We've got a breech delivery. Mrs. Bulloch."

He opened his eyes. "Jean Bulloch? You're kidding me. This afternoon she was in wonderful condition. What happened?"

"Damned if I know."

"All right, Jim. Hang in there. I'll be at the hospital in"—he looked at the clock glowing on the nightstand and sighed—"say, thirty minutes. Hold her."

Josh handed the phone back to his wife and pushed the covers off. He crawled out of bed and stood, flexing the pain out of his back.

"What is going on over there?" Pat asked. She was up on her elbow now, shielding her eyes from the bedside light he had just snapped on.

"Mrs. Bulloch's in labor. An unexpected breech. No time for a C-section. This is ridiculous."

"Not that ridiculous," she said to his back as he stumbled toward the bathroom. "Is something wrong with your equipment over there? Or maybe it's the city water? How many premature births does this town get in five months? Going for the *Guinness Book of Records?*" She shouted to the closing door.

After he had quickly showered and changed, Josh slipped into his daughter's room, where yellow curtains billowed in the Gulf breeze. Amy lay on her back with her mouth open. Her light brown hair lay soft against the pillow. So beautiful, he thought, my little girl. He tiptoed across the floor—careful not to step on any of the dozens of toys that squawked, burped, and giggled—and kissed his daughter on the forehead. "I love you," he whispered. She wrinkled her nose and blew a puff of air out of her small bow-shaped mouth. What a wonder she was, he thought to himself, at nine, the very beginning of her life. Then he thought about Jean Bulloch, who was fighting for her own life and the life of her unborn baby.

Josh hurried from the house and took the beach road up toward Clearwater and the bridge that would bring him to Tampa Memorial. The Gulf of Mexico was calm after a week of storms. The moon penciled its way across the sea. So quiet, so tranquil, at this time of morning. Waves lapped against the shore; beach condos loomed up like silent monolithic sentries guarding the shore. Along the inland side of the road were small restaurants, stucco apartment buildings, and clapboard homes built before World War II. He loved it here on Florida's west coast where the weather, guided by the Gulf Stream, seldom varied. The world was clean and bright and hopeful, especially for the elderly who had come here for their final peace. Of course, this area also had the fastest-growing birth rate in the nation, which for an ob-gyn was financial paradise.

He had said good-bye to Cleveland after completing his internship, good-bye to the dreariness and the stifled inhabitants for whom the body seemed necessary only to carry around the head. It was too cerebral, too depressing, too disembodied for him. His mother and father had worked hard and died young so that their only child could do something with his life. He had finally left, he supposed, out of fear that he would end up the same way. He had left to build a life with Pat and Amy, but lately he had begun to wonder. With all the problems lately, the passion seemed to have vanished. He and Pat were drifting apart.

The last few months had been depressing. Everything between them had changed. A great many of their troubles had to do with the hospital and the chaos there. Premature births. Deformed babies. Late-night calls. Screwed-up computers. A goddamn madhouse. Josh wanted to believe that pure bad fortune was at the root of the problems; there was no other explanation. He had even called other doctors in the Tampa Bay area, looking for a local pattern to explain his misfortune, but he'd found nothing out of the ordinary. Had to be bad luck. But why him? And why so much of it?

He pulled into the Tampa Memorial staff parking lot and eased the Oldsmobile into its slot. The hospital was quiet, except for his ward, where two nurses and Jim Ellison greeted him at the desk with coffee, bug eyes, and worried looks.

"How bad is it?" he asked Jim, who was eight years younger than he and had been his associate for two years. Josh had hired him on the spot when he discovered his Harvard Medical School background, Mayo Clinic internship, and residency at Bellevue in New York. Ellison was clearly a superior doctor as well as a compassionate young man.

Jim Ellison was upset. He said, "She's worse, and frankly I don't know what to make of it."

After scrubbing, Josh went inside, where he slipped into a sterile gown and gloves. The delivery room nurse had completed the prep and drape routine. He could see the baby's buttocks expanding the vaginal opening while the nurse encouraged Jean to push. Josh knew the baby's legs were bent up against its abdomen and chest and would have to be released as soon as the buttocks were free enough to allow him a firm grasp.

"Come on, now," he said, easing the legs out. Next he flexed the arms and tried to deliver them, along with the shoulders. Trouble. The baby was lodged in such a way that the shoulders refused to give. Josh pulled and twisted at various angles, but there was no give. Time was suddenly against him.

"Help me out, Jean," he said to the woman who writhed on the table. Josh was feeling her pain. He finally pulled the arms, shoulders, and head free, but

11

the baby had been without oxygen for too long. The umbilical cord carrying the blood supply had been compressed, clamping it off.

The baby was limp and pale and made no effort to breathe on its own. The heart rate was too slow. It had half-closed milky green eyes and tufts of wet red hair, and its skin was covered with sores. Josh moved the baby to the warmer and gave it oxygen while compressing and releasing its chest. "Come on, little guy," he pleaded.

Josh waited, hoping that the baby would breathe on its own. "Call Dr. Tucker," he said to the nurse. *"Stat!"*

Tucker was the pediatrician on duty. Josh grabbed the laryngoscope, inserted the plastic airway into the baby's trachea, and pumped oxygen directly into the lungs. The color and heart rate improved, but the baby was still flaccid; there was no sign of breathing.

"Sodium bicarbonate," he said to the nurse, who stood over the baby, looking into its face, transfixed. "I'm trying to prevent acidosis here."

The nurse snapped to attention and handed him the needle, which he injected into the child's behind.

Dr. Gert Tucker, blond hair tucked out of sight, entered the room. "Take care of Mom, Josh," she said. "I'll handle it here."

"Tough breech, Gert," Josh said, moving to the mother.

Just then the baby moved—a jerk, a sputter, then a feeble gasp. Gert removed the tracheal tube, and the baby gave out a weak cry, trying to breathe.

"Come to the nursery when you're through here,"

Gert said to Josh and carried the baby out of the room.

Josh said a few words to a stabilizing Jean Bulloch, then left her with Jim Ellison and the nurse. He walked down the corridor and into the nursery, where he found Gert, who had put the baby on the ventilation machine and I.V. fluids. The lab technician drew blood samples.

"Let's go to the call room." Gert led Josh out, and when they were alone, she said, "The child's going to live, but it has poor muscle tone, and you know what a bad sign that is. There's going to be significant brain damage, possible cerebral palsy."

"Jesus."

"And did you notice the coloring and the epidermal sores?"

"Could be a virus of some kind." Josh leaned against a table. "I don't have any excuses. The baby should have been sectioned, but there wasn't time." He didn't know what else to say. He looked up at Gert, who was waiting for him to speak. "The parents have to be told," he said finally, "I'll do it." As he left for the waiting room a familiar fear rose up in him. Another one, he thought. Would this bad luck never end?

At seven-thirty Josh called Pat from the office, apologizing once again for the early-morning pyrotechnics. He got angry whenever he felt the need to explain these things. She understood what life as a doctor was about. Had she forgotten all those years when he had to get up at dawn during his medical training? The internship, residency, and first years of practice had been tough, too, but he and Pat had worked together, struggled, and dreamed. He suddenly felt guilty for taking his anger out on her.

A hand reached out and grabbed him; he snapped his arm away. Jim took hold of him and pinned him in a mock half nelson.

"You get pissy with me again, boy," Jim said, "and I'm going to break your arm so you can't operate for a while—just to get you off my back."

"That bad, huh?"

Jim threw out his arms. "Who, you? Why, you're the nicest guy in the world . . . when you're asleep. Yeah, you've been a royal pain in the ass the last few weeks, if you wanna know the truth."

"Living inside the body of a crank is no great joy, either, let me tell you."

"You're going to have to say that to the other fifty people you've been terrorizing." Jim laughed and offered him a cup of coffee. "Hey, everybody understands. It's the rotation system. Sucks!" Jim leaned back against the counter and crossed his arms. "I'm going to prescribe serious bed rest, and you tell Pat she owes you one long massage."

Josh smiled weakly, wondering what the chance of that would be. He and Pat loved each other, he was sure of that. But sometimes love was not enough. Sometimes he looked down the line and envisioned horrible fights, separation, even divorce. A grim prognosis. He was too tired to fight. Something had to break; some of the pressure had to drain off.

He took the chart for his next patient and carried

it into his office, closing the door behind him. He decided to take a catnap.

Thirty seconds later the phone rang. It was Mrs. Burleson, in the grips of an anxiety attack about her pregnancy. The image of Jean Bulloch and her child filled his mind.

"Yes, Mrs. Burleson," he said, his hand shaking, "what is it?"

2

PAT SWITCHED ON HER FAVORITE COUNTRY MUSIC STATION as she aimed the station wagon toward the beach. She had just dropped Amy off at school and was on her way to the *St. Petersburg Herald* offices to meet with her editor, Harold Carey. It was already nine, and she knew she'd never make it on time. Harold would holler something about how there ought to be a law forbidding mothers to work as journalists. Or maybe he would threaten her with an assignment for the society pages. She imagined him waving Section C menacingly in front of her and shouting, "Is ten o'clock too early for a working mother? A women's club is holding an afternoon symposium on diet pills and the divorced woman. Like to cover that instead?"

For all his ranting, Harold was one of the few people who had stood by her. There hadn't been many women reporting on health care issues six years ago, especially women without medical degrees. Harold had taken a chance on her, even encouraged her to carve a niche for herself in the male-dominated field. He'd let her research and write the first articles on DES babies, and she returned the favor by getting the paper its first award for medical reporting.

Of course it was Josh who had made that first award possible. Without his help, she could never have written with the medical insight of a professional doctor. She remembered how he had spent hours with her every evening, giving her a crash course in gynecology and directing her to the most useful publications. She knew that she owed a large measure of her success to him. No other beginning medical reporter had quite her inside edge. Few writers were married to a doctor who was willing to go over every word they wrote.

When had that stopped? Pat asked herself. It had been years since Josh had read one of her articles, even after publication. He no longer checked her preliminary drafts or directed her to sources. After six years with the *Herald* she knew where to look when she needed accurate information.

She turned the radio off; the country music was beginning to grate on her nerves. How could she feel lonely with a brilliant husband, a beautiful daughter, and a career she wanted and loved? She knew too many women who were single or childless not to be thankful for her family. But being thankful did not drive any of the sorrow away.

Maybe we started with too much, she told herself. She had met Josh when he was a first-year medical student at the University of Florida and she was auditing courses at the med school as a graduate student in journalism. Her emphasis was on medical reporting, the ideal way for a doctor's daughter to combine a talent for writing with a long-standing interest in medicine. Second best to the real thing, she had assured her father.

Pat and Josh had found each other during the second semester. Josh had had his eye on the "only beautiful girl" in the class, while Pat had wondered how to meet the aloof but "quietly devastating" boy who shyly reeled off perfect answers—but only when called upon.

It was Josh's roommate who finally brought them together by simply introducing them at the library one day. After an hour of hushed chatter amid the stacks they had decided to continue the conversation at a coffee shop. Then at a restaurant, a bar, and finally in Josh's apartment. He asked her to marry him a week later; it was that simple, that right.

It wasn't that right anymore, Pat thought, and yet she knew it wasn't exactly wrong, either. He had a grueling work schedule; she had a demanding job and a daughter. So many things were wedged between them, and they were, for the most part, things they wanted and loved. Family and careers. They could no longer live in the hazy bliss of love; their worlds had expanded too much for that.

Pat took the Park Street exit and checked the time. Fifteen minutes late already. She would not reach the paper for another twenty. She felt a vague hankering for a drink, just a little one to calm her nerves. Not a good sign. She knew she had been drinking too much lately, but there were just too many nights without Josh.

Now she thought that a vodka gimlet might really take the edge off being late. She hated the idea that other reporters were late because they had slept in, while she had to get up at six and rush to get Amy off for school. She reminded herself that the world was not fair and that she had things other women would envy. The gimlet could wait.

Pat was relieved when Harold greeted her with a warm smile and ushered her into his office.

"Sorry I'm late," she said. "It was my daughter—"

"Don't remind me of your maternal duties," he said. "I've got something special for you."

Pat felt the charge of adrenaline that always accompanied a new assignment. She grabbed her notebook and pen. "What is it?"

Harold grinned mutely.

"Come on, Harold, you said special—what?"

The wicked grin broadened. "Bill Walters and I were having a chat."

Harold and the publisher were having a chat about her? Pat could feel her skin prickle.

"We might have a job for you."

"An assignment? An article?" Pat practically shouted in exasperation.

He leaned forward and whispered the magical words: "A series."

Pat gasped. Her first series. No matter how sharp any of her individual articles were, none would get the attention that a series would bring. She had submitted several ideas for series. Most of them had been rejected, and some were modified only to be handed over to other reporters.

"You want to sit gaping or you want to ask what it is?" Harold teased.

"A weekly series?" Pat asked.

He nodded.

"For how long?"

"Six weeks."

"Bingo!" she cried.

The subject, Harold explained, was controversial and of particular interest to readers in the Tampa Bay–St. Petersburg area, which would be greatly affected, especially the elderly population.

"Specifically?" Pat said, trying to remain calm.

"Corporate sponsorship of genetic research," Harold said. Several crucial gains had been made in the field as a result of funding from major corporations, he went on to say. What role did the companies play in determining what was being researched? Was the government beginning to rely on corporate backing to take the place of federal funding for the sciences?

"The Senate vote coming up will have an enormous impact," Harold said. "And we want to present all sides of the issue."

Pat was aware of the issues. She had read about legal battles over FDA approvals and federal clearances, and Josh had mentioned some of the genetic breakthroughs that were beginning to affect obstetricians.

"Are you taking the position that the companies are

doing more for the development of the science than the government agencies?" Pat asked.

"I'm not taking any position yet. I'm giving you the topic. It's up to you to find out what you can."

"I've heard that some of the companies are doing genetic research experiments without FDA sanction. Because they have the money to foot the bills, they're getting away with highly questionable research practices."

"I'm delighted that you've got some background on the issues," he said, "but I don't give two cents for anything you've heard, even from that hotshot husband of yours. Back it up."

"I always back up my stories," Pat snapped. "You know that."

"That's one of the reasons I'm letting you have this. And also because you've been doing exceptional work over the past two years. It's your time to shine with a series."

As Harold went over the project, Pat realized that she had been given a gem. This was cutting-edge material, the perfect story for a reporter with visions of Pulitzers in her head. She was flattered and more than a little puzzled that Harold was entrusting her with a series of this scope.

"What about Frank?" Pat asked. Frank Bund was the paper's senior medical reporter, and even though she was next in line, the older reporter seemed to go out of his way to make sure she was never given a really choice assignment.

"Frank? Is there something wrong with you, lady?" Harold said. "I give you the best damn story you've ever had and you want to know why I didn't give it to someone else?"

Pat's training asserted itself. "If I'm going to do this right," she said, "I want to make sure I'm not being handed this series for any reason other than that I'm the reporter who's best qualified to write it. I'm not interested in political maneuverings between you and Frank, me and Frank, or Frank and the entire medical community."

Harold got out of his chair and stood behind his desk. That's it, Pat thought, I've gone too far.

"And I'm not interested in giving important assignments to anyone who isn't capable of doing top work."

"What does that mean?"

"It means don't ever question my motives for choosing a reporter."

"I can handle the series."

"That's why I called you in here. Don't waste my time on this shit again." The words were tough, but the old smirk reappeared as he shoved a pile of loose papers into her arms. "These are just to get you going. Reports, contact names, a list of FDA rulings. I want you on this full time."

Full time. Pat thought of Josh, Amy, the thousand petty errands that needed doing. It would be a crunch, but she had not felt this excited or energetic in a long time. Against all newsroom etiquette, Pat leaned over and gave Harold a big kiss on the cheek.

3

DR. DAVID MORRIS SAT IN THE LIBRARY OF HIS FALL Springs, Indiana, home, wondering what his medical school buddies would think of him now. A failure. The man once heralded as the most promising young doctor in his class was now a monumental flop. Everything—his practice, his family, his integrity— was on the brink of ruin, and it was all his fault.

The gray sky outside the window was a perfect reflection of the way he felt. He had been staring at it, and at the Indiana cornfields, for hours. He did not, as a rule, drink in the afternoon, but today he felt the need. A dozen medical books lay on the desk before him, next to the bottle of scotch. He had been scouring the texts, hoping to find some medical reason why things had been going wrong. Mary Wills's death was still inconceivable to him. There was no explanation, medical or otherwise, why she had died—at least none that he knew.

A Mozart piano concerto played in the background. He took his eyes away from the window and looked at his hands folded in front of him. They were wrinkled and scarred and could easily have belonged to a man much older than he. He reached for the scotch and poured another drink.

Was it time to draw up another list of recent disasters? Why not? He pulled out a notebook and started. First, there was his practice—what there was left of it. Word was out that strange things were going on in Dr. Morris's office, and a lot of women were looking for a new obstetrician.

So many births had involved major complications of one kind or another. His sleeping habits were shot from too many emergency phone calls at three in the morning. During the past few weeks he had dreaded going to the office for fear of what he would have to face. He had been canceling appointments or referring his patients to his young partner, Ben Brost.

Thank God for Ben. David felt lucky to have him. Ben was reliable, always there, uncomplaining, and efficient. On occasion David found himself worrying that Ben might be offered a more sophisticated practice in the city.

David swung his chair around and faced the fireplace. Above the mantelpiece was a painting of his grandfather, Dr. David Morris the first. Number One, as they all called him. "Sorry, One," he said, holding up his glass. He felt awful about having let Granddad down. He was letting everyone down—his grandfather, his children, and especially his wife. Poor Melanie. What had he done to her?

He had never even looked at another woman, and now this. He still could not explain what had happened, why he had allowed himself to become involved with Sarah.

He closed his eyes and created a mental vision of Sarah: her milk-white skin, her jade-colored eyes, the luxuriant red hair that fell over her shoulders, and the exquisite, long body that drove him mad. She had become an obsession with him. He was over his head in love, or was it lust? He had been seized by her, gobbled up, dominated, sucked in. On top of that, he was insanely jealous, an emotion he had not believed was in him. He demanded to know where she went when she vanished for days on end. He felt as if he were under her spell, but he knew it was a spell of his own making. He hated the feeling, but he couldn't let her go. Wanting her—*craving* her, really—was destroying everything it had taken him years to build, including his marriage. He loved Melanie more than ever, so why couldn't he let go of Sarah? He drained his glass and poured another drink.

The children were suffering. This longing for Sarah was like a cancer; it insinuated itself into everything he did. "Stop it!" he shouted over the music. "Please! Stop this!"

He felt light-headed. He put his drink down and tried to stand, but lost his balance and reached for the edge of the desk. *Sarah.* Even the name left him with an ache. She had come in with those long legs and that smile, that sex of hers. What a number she had pulled on him.

This was not love but a sickness. "God help me," he

said, falling back in the chair and cupping his head in his hands.

He heard a noise in the other room. He remembered that Melanie was at the zoo with the kids. His watch read 3:30, much too early for her to return. He would have to sober up before they got back. He picked up the bottle and saw that it was already half gone—just as he was.

There was the noise again. Creaking footsteps? He stood up and aimed his body at the door. "All right," he said, "I'm coming."

He had taken a couple of wobbly steps forward when the library door swung open.

"Hey!" he said. "What brings you here? Sit down. Have a drink." He laughed and added, "I've had a few already, but you may be able to persuade me to join you."

As he leaned back to get the bottle and another glass, he felt the hands on him. "Hey," he said, "I'll be all right. Just take me a second to fix this for you. You drink scotch, right? Of course you do. You know, I was thinking about you earlier today, and there is something I must talk to you about. Christ, I have to talk to somebody about it before I go completely mad."

David sat in the chair and took the bottle of scotch from the table. But the bottle was taken out of his hands and he was eased back into the chair.

He felt a handkerchief against his forehead. "Thank you," he said, giving himself over to the gentleness.

"I have been in such turmoil," David said, "you can't imagine."

His arms were placed on the armrests, and one

sleeve of his shirt was being rolled up. "The pressure on me has been so great, I just don't know what to do. You understand all that. Of course you do. If anyone does, it's you."

David didn't understand why a cotton ball soaked with alcohol was being rubbed over a vein in his arm. He wasn't sick, as far as he knew; then again, maybe he was.

"I'll have to get at this first thing in the morning. We cannot let this wait. The entire practice is in jeopardy."

He still felt light-headed from the scotch, and he needed to sober up. Maybe a shot was just what he needed. Anything to relieve his pain.

"Okay," he heard himself say, "first thing in the morning," and he closed his eyes.

4

"WHEN WAS THE FIRST DAY OF YOUR LAST PERIOD?" JULIE Palmer asked.

"January twenty-seventh," Kelly Cox replied, "I'm sure because we left for vacation that day, and I was annoyed."

Julie checked a date wheel. "Then you'd be just five weeks pregnant if you test positive."

Kelly Cox had always found Julie, Dr. Heller's office assistant, a little scary—the woman was large and very stern. But today Julie's gruffness seemed reassuring. After all, there was no nonsense about having a child.

"I know! I've counted it all out." Kelly could not keep the excitement out of her voice. She had been trying to have a child for a year without so much as missing a period. Now she was over a week late.

"The blood test result won't be in until this afternoon, but Dr. Ellison is going to examine you this morning."

"That's fine." Dr. Heller was Kelly's regular doctor, but Dr. Ellison sometimes did routine examinations. She liked him well enough. Today she would have let Julie examine her if it meant she would find out she was pregnant that much sooner.

Dr. Jim Ellison's short blond hair and square jaw made him look like an all-American jock of about thirty-five. He hung up the phone and went to greet his next patient. He ushered her into one of the offices and left her to strip from the waist down. After a moment he knocked at the examining room door. "All set?"

"Ready," Kelly called through the door.

Dr. Ellison had her lie back on the table and carefully draped the sheet over her raised legs.

"The cervix looks healthy," he said as he began to probe gently inside. "The uterus is flexible, and if I'm not mistaken, ever so slightly extended."

Kelly gasped happily in disbelief. "You mean . . . ?"

"Nothing certain until your blood test result is in, but I'd venture that there's a good chance you've got a little friend in there."

Kelly sat up on the table, "Oh, thank you," she gushed. "Can you believe . . . a baby!"

"Not so fast," Jim said, laughing, "we're in the middle of an examination here." Kelly lay down obediently and waited for him to proceed.

"I'm just taking a small sample, like a Pap smear, nothing to worry about. You're going to feel a little pinch."

Kelly liked the way both doctors always told her exactly what they were doing. The white sheet hid whatever procedures went on beneath it, so it was comforting to know what to expect.

Now Kelly felt the small pinch—nothing, really—and watched as Dr. Ellison withdrew a thin instrument, touched it to a sheet of glass, covered and labeled the sample, and placed it in a refrigerated box.

"Great," he told her. "You can get dressed now. If you test positive, I want you to make an appointment with me right away."

"Of course," Kelly said, "but what about Dr. Heller?"

"Dr. Heller has a busy schedule right now, so I'll see you for the first exam. We'll talk about nutrition and get you some vitamins. Routine stuff. After that, you'll be back in Dr. Heller's capable hands. Okay?"

Kelly flushed. She had not meant to insult Dr. Ellison. "It's just . . . he's been my doctor for years."

Dr. Ellison smiled warmly at her. "Of course. But can you tell me why he gets all the nicest patients?"

Kelly laughed as the doctor left her. Inside, she was sure, there was a little baby laughing, too.

Dr. Josh Heller nearly collided with the young Chinese man who darted out of Jim Ellison's office and down the hallway. "Hey!" Josh shouted, but found his rebuke cut short by the man's charming smile as he slowed and said, "Excuse me, Dr. Heller."

He executed a small half bow and continued down the hallway carrying a small metal box.

Josh was surprised that the young man knew who he was. He was not the usual delivery boy, but they did tend to change every few months. Josh guessed that he had probably seen this man twenty times in the past few weeks but had been too preoccupied to notice.

He felt out of touch with so many elements of his office practice now. The young man had already disappeared down the stairwell exit when Josh felt a wave of exhaustion break over him. He braced himself against the door frame, waiting for it to pass.

He had been called to the hospital at four in the morning. By ten he had lost his third premature delivery of the month. It was ten-thirty now, and he faced a backlog of patient calls and office work. He wanted to go home and go to sleep. Jim could cover for him, and then with a few hours of solid rest under his belt, things around here might not look so bleak. He had stepped back from the doorway, ready to call it a day, when he heard banging coming from inside his office.

"What in hell . . ." He opened the door and saw Julie waging a full bodily attack on the computer terminal behind the main reception area. At six feet, a hundred sixty pounds, she looked as though she might just succeed in tearing the screen off the monitor face.

"Computer problems or is this a new aerobic work-out? Julie, what's going on?"

"Aerobics my ass," Julie grunted and she gave the screen another jab. "If this thing had any decency it would curl up and die. Look at these." She handed

Josh a printout of some recent patient histories, all hopelessly jumbled by odd symbols and misplaced numbers.

"When did this start?" he said to her, holding up the mess.

"There were problems yesterday, today's been impossible, and you've been needing a new system for almost a year."

What she said was true. They had been talking about replacing the old machines, but no one had done much about it. "Go easy," Josh said. "I'm swamped as it is."

"You better believe it." She handed him a stack of phone messages. "These are the easy ones, pal, but, hey"—she patted his arm—"we'll get through them."

Amazing how gentle the giant could be, he thought to himself. Right now, her tawny eyes widened with sympathy. She looked so reassuring—the perfect shoulder to cry on. Josh felt some of his energy returning.

"Let's do the calls first," he said as he led the way into his office. "Then we'll deal with the machine."

Julie dropped the list of calls on his desk: a bladder infection, a request to speak at a childbirth class, a question about sterilization. This was business as usual, small problems, common worries. With Julie he knew that he could handle them. This was a part of the morning routine that used to annoy him. Most of the calls were uninteresting, symptomatic of anxiety rather than real trouble. He hated the telephone and preferred to spend time with his patients face to face.

Yet today, after a week of tragedies, he relished the

mundane questions and routine prescriptions. It was easier to appreciate the simple things after you'd been thrown ten dozen curve balls. Josh hoped that by next week he would be blissfully annoyed by the dreary and the humdrum.

The calm was broken a few minutes later when Julie screamed from the other room. "That's it! I've had it!"

"What?"

She stormed into Josh's office with sheets of computer paper trailing behind her, brushed by him, and stomped through the door into the next room. Josh got out of his chair and followed her.

Julie hovered over the computer, hair dangling in her face, scowling. "Either we've lost a chip or somebody's been screwing around with this thing." She blew the hair out of her eyes and punched in a patient's name: Joan Arnold. "Watch this," she said.

The information on Joan materialized: her address, phone number, and social security number were all there. Julie pressed "return," and a list of Joan's visits, in chronological order, appeared on the screen, along with relevant medical information, test results, and drug prescriptions.

"Right here," Julie said as she pointed to the last six months' visit records. "Joan's first visit this year was in February—you see? The data's all scrambled, and I know some of this stuff isn't right. It says here she was in for a biopsy when I know that she was only in for a routine exam."

"How's this possible? How could the data be wrong? I remember Joan's visit, and you're right about the biopsy." He thought for a minute and asked, "Are you sure the data was entered correctly?"

"Josh," Julie told him, "I did it myself. I never make that kind of mistake."

She looked so insulted that Josh said quickly, "I'm sorry, Julie, I know your work is flawless. It's just that it would be easier to deal with, not to mention less expensive, if it was just a human error."

"It's okay. I know the last thing you need is another problem, but it looks like we've got one. The weird thing is, it seems to be random misordering. It looks to me like the file information is normal for some patients and all mixed up for others."

"We've got backups?" Josh asked.

"Sure, but that's no good if the information on them is wrong, too, or if the data we put in from now on will be scrambled."

"Okay," Josh said, sighing, "we begin the computer search in earnest. Maybe we'll call the computer guy and go with whatever he has to offer. I don't think we've got time to shop around."

"Right, boss," Julie said. "And don't worry, things are bound to ease up." She shooed him back toward his office as the phone rang. He heard her talking cheerfully to a patient as he headed to the examining room, already late.

That morning Josh saw twenty patients, back to back. He was used to busy days, and it felt good to see women with standard cases. Only three were pregnant, and so far all of them appeared to be perfectly normal pregnancies. It was after one o'clock when Josh stopped for lunch.

They had a small kitchen set up in a back room, a half-size refrigerator, a sink, and a microwave, and it was a godsend on busy days. Josh made it a policy to bring in any dinner leftovers for the next day's lunch. Pat was a great cook, and most nights she prepared extra servings so that there would be enough to feed him, Jim, and Julie.

Jim was already at the microwave when Josh walked into the kitchen. Without Pat's lunches, Josh knew Jim would be feeding on SpaghettiOs and Pop-Tarts, which he referred to as soul food.

"Ah, Doctor, do sit down." Jim bowed gracefully and gestured to the table. "Today Chez Heller is serving . . . ah, looks like white meat in soupy sauce."

"That happens to be chicken Véronique."

"Like I said, cheekeen veroonique, the pride of the Florida French." Jim dunked a finger into the sauce and slurped. "Mmmm-mmmm. Your lovely wife would make a fine addition to my pathetic bachelor kitchen, should you be inclined to loan her."

"Sorry, pal, you're going to have to make do with leftovers."

Jim brought two plates heaped with sauced chicken and wild rice to the table. "This meal is crying out for a Pepsi. Care to join me?" He plopped two unopened cans on the table.

"At least you don't shake them anymore," said Josh.

They ate quickly, exchanging grunts until the food

was gone. They were always comfortable with each other. Josh enjoyed Jim's easy manner and small pranks. He was the most unflappable man Josh had ever met, always smiling and cool, even in the middle of the most harrowing deliveries. Josh often wondered if anything ever upset Jim. He seemed to be one of those people who mysteriously escaped bad fortune. Josh could not recall ever seeing him sweat, nor could he remember Jim being moody. It was a minor miracle to have a business partner without troubles.

"Didn't you mention seeing a computer demo a few weeks back?" Josh said to him.

Jim scrunched up his face thoughtfully. "I talked to some guy, but to tell you the truth I'm not sure what I saw. Computers don't make sense to me."

"We've got two computer-stupid people in this room."

"He did leave a price list and some printed information," Jim said. "Will that help?"

Josh nodded. "It might." Jim left to hunt for the material and returned with a small glossy brochure. All the basic information was there: the hardware setup, monitors, printer, the standard $10,000 price tag.

"Okay, I'll take care of it," Josh said, glancing at the brochure. "This looks about as good as anything else I've seen."

"It's not too much money?"

"It's not cheap, but that's what they all cost, give or take a few hundred."

Jim cocked his head and said, "You know, I just remembered some other stuff I got. Hang on for a

36

minute." He disappeared again and returned with a crumpled piece of paper. "This came from a med school buddy of mine who said the equipment was first class and cheap."

Josh smoothed out the paper and read aloud: "'Adams Computer. Sam Adams, President.' Sam Adams? I can just hear this guy's buy-American pitch." He glanced up at Julie, who entered the room looking as if she was ready to detonate a bomb under the machine.

"What the hell?" he said. "I'll call old Sam. What've we got to lose?"

5

At noon the door to Josh's office opened and Julie walked in acting strangely. Her face was red, and her lips were tightly pursed. She seemed to be blowing up like an inner tube, trying to hold something in. She avoided his eyes as she lumbered over and deposited on his desk a white business card that read: SAM ADAMS. ADAMS COMPUTER COMPANY. No address or telephone number.

"Sam's in the waiting room," she said, the words flowing sweetly out of her mouth.

"Wonderful. Why don't you show him in?" Josh caught something in her expression. "Are you all right?"

Julie couldn't hold it in any longer, and the laughter burst right out of her. "Oh, I'm fantastic," she said when she was able to speak. "Everything's just peachy, you'll see."

Josh stared at her, wondering what was going on. "Julie?"

"What?"

"Underneath all that efficiency you're crazy, aren't you?"

She laughed at that, too, and then spun around on the balls of her feet and left the room. A second later she was back. "Oh, Dr. Heller," he heard her say from the doorway. "I'd like you to meet Sam Adams, who is here to see you about the computer equipment."

Josh made a final notation in the daybook and looked up. He was not prepared for the figure he saw standing beside Julie—a voluptuous woman who stood at least five-eight, with milky skin, long red hair, and almond-shaped green eyes. She was a knockout. She wore a conservative green dress just a shade lighter than her eyes.

"I'll be right outside if you need me, Doctor," Julie said. "Your jaw medicine is in the upper right-hand drawer."

"My jaw med . . ." Josh got out of his chair and walked around his desk. "Thank you, Julie," he said and closed the door behind her.

"Dr. Heller." The woman extended her hand. "Samantha Adams." Josh shook the perfectly mani-cured hand and led her to a chair.

"Excuse me if I seem a little surprised," he said to her, "but I was expecting a zealous patriot wearing a red, white, and blue tie."

She smiled at him and unlocked her attaché case, pulled out a sheaf of papers, and placed it on his desk.

"I suppose I am overzealous about my business," she said, "and patriotic. You were just wrong about the tie."

Josh watched as she neatly arranged the papers. Her movements were very exact, but with a kind of childlike intensity, as if she had to concentrate to make the simplest gestures. A perfectionist, he thought to himself, probably way too hard on herself.

"I'm sure you've looked at other systems," she said, getting down to business.

"We have all the brochures. They all look the same, same price, slightly different design. Who knows?" He found himself feeling uncomfortable with this shockingly gorgeous woman.

"I'll tell you right up front that Adams's equipment is not that different from that of the other companies. But I can offer you service features engineered with a doctor's office in mind—at a better than usual price. Why don't you take a look at this?" She slid the material across the desk toward Josh. "There's a twenty-megabyte hard drive, and we provide all the software. The program we've designed will handle patient accounts and billing, insurance, history and physical examination records, spread and balance sheets, payroll, and taxes."

Her speaking voice was intriguing, and yet there was a hollowness to it. She spoke with no inflection, like a prep school girl who never moved her lips, and she had a trace of an accent. He noticed other odd things, too. For one, when she spoke she locked her eyes on his and kept them there without blinking, which made him self-conscious. After a while he suggested they head down to the hospital cafeteria for lunch.

"I've already made reservations at the Harbor Inn," she replied. "Unless you'd rather not."

"Harbor Inn?" The most expensive place on the beach. "I'd love to," he said.

Out in the parking lot she insisted on taking her car, so he climbed into the passenger side of her late-model Jaguar. Along the way he began to appreciate the take-charge thoroughness of Samantha Adams.

The restaurant was on the shore of a broad water-way with large bleached-white mansions lining the seawalls. To the west the canal fed out into the calm silver waters of the Gulf of Mexico. The day was like any other in this bastion of subtropical ennui—bright, humid, and hot.

To enter the Harbor Inn they walked under a bower of palm fronds and through a heavy wooden door with a scrolled "H.I." emblazoned across a coat of arms. All very tasteful, this snug, well-appointed place. The hostess who led them to their table wore a simple white dress, flamingo earrings, and nail polish the color of sand.

As soon as they got inside Josh saw heads turn in their direction—actually, in Samantha's direction. Both men and women ogled and gawked. After their initial dazzlement wore off, they focused on the man with her. "Hi, Renner," Josh said to Renner Mohl, chief of surgery at St. Pete General. Josh greeted John Mashek, who owned the marina and from whom he had bought his Bay Cruiser, and Sandy Bonner who had cut the deal at the bank. Their appraisal of

Samantha made Josh feel awkward, as if he was expected to explain what he was doing with her. What was a five-foot-ten-inch regular looking guy of forty-four doing with the bombshell of America? He didn't like the way it made him feel—as if he was out of his league, or guilty.

He asked the waitress to seat them away from everyone else, in the garden room. Josh ordered for both of them.

During lunch he found himself putting her under a microscope. It was obvious that she was gorgeous, but there was more. He remembered from school a line out of D. H. Lawrence in which he described one of his characters as having an "intrinsic otherness."

She told him about being raised and educated in Washington, D.C., and about Adams Computer, which she started with money she had made from investments. She rented office space and a home in Tampa, but spent a lot of her time traveling to other locations, trying to keep her customers happy and her overhead down.

"You're on the road a lot, then?" he said.

She looked up quickly at him and lowered her eyes. "Yes, too much."

"What does that do to your social life?"

"What social life?"

"You must have somebody."

She stared into her lap and pressed her lips together. He was getting too personal for a business lunch and told himself to stop it.

"There was somebody," she said, "but he's gone,

42

and I suppose with all the traveling, I've kept myself too busy to think about it."

"I'm sorry," Josh said.

"No, that's all right. You have a good bedside manner." She glanced up at him and smiled. "When you own your own business and are always on the go, you don't make friends and you can't keep lovers."

"Do you have family? Your parents?"

"They died when I was young," she said and added, "I hope I don't sound as if I'm complaining too much. I actually like my life, and it's really not out of Dickens. What about you? Let's see . . . I'll bet you have a family. And you have at least one child and a very smart wife."

"One great kid and one smart wife."

"She's lucky to have you. They both are. You're a very nice man."

Josh arched his eyebrows and looked over at her with a mock-evil grin. "You don't know me very well."

"On the contrary, I believe I do." She reached over and patted his hand. "We all have small problems, but with effort they get solved." She left her hand on top of his. "And I think if we don't get back to your office you won't have any patients left, and you won't need my computer equipment anymore."

Josh had hardly touched his food.

Later in his office Josh agreed that the following Wednesday would be the best time for a demonstration.

"You should know," Samantha said, "that I'll include a one-year service contract and, at no extra charge, a personal unit for your office. The total cost will be six thousand dollars."

"Six?" A little more than half of what the other computer companies wanted.

"A fair price, don't you think?"

"I'd say. How can you come in that low?"

"I keep my supplier confidential, but I can promise you that the quality is as good as anyone's. So, Dr. Heller, you can see . . ."

"Please call me Josh."

"That's a lovely name. Josh. Rugged but compassionate. Like a character out of the old West."

"That's me. Just a cowboy."

"Well, it's been very nice meeting you, Dr. Heller," she said. "Josh. See you on Wednesday." Before he could do more than nod, she had the attaché case under her arm and was walking out the door.

"Some lunch," Julie said, looking at her watch. "Two hours."

"No cracks."

Julie tousled her hair and struck a pinup pose. "Whatever do you mean, Dr. Heller—Josh?"

Josh looked over Julie's shoulder into the waiting room where half a dozen patients sat reading magazines. He was way behind schedule. "Give me a couple of minutes," he said to Julie, who left, closing the door behind her. He sat back in his chair and swiveled around to look out the window and across the lot filled with sand spurs to the waterway.

Samantha Adams was a strange one—on the outside an aggressive young business woman, on the inside vulnerable, like a child. He liked her, mainly because she tried hard and seemed driven, the kind who refused to buckle under. He admired her spirit. He remembered when he and Pat were her age and the spirit they had back then. A heavy depression fell over him and he quickly shut his eyes against it.

Pressing his fingers to his temples, he took a number of deep breaths and forced himself to concentrate on the air as he inhaled and exhaled—a Japanese breathing exercise he learned a long time ago when he took an aikido class. After a moment he felt calm, back in touch. He reached over and pressed the intercom. "Okay, Julie," he said. "Run them dogies in."

"What?"

"Just an old cowboy expression."

6

Washington, D.C.

U.S. SENATOR CURT MANHEIM FINISHED READING HIS fourth newspaper of the day, the *Los Angeles Times*, and stared at the fish in the tank his daughter had given him many years ago. The tank was oval-shaped and sat like a big bubble on a table in the center of his office. Fish. "Pretend they're pets, Daddy," Rebecca had instructed him. Pet fish.

Manheim picked up a porcelain egg, another gift from his daughter, and rolled it around in his fingers. She called it his worry egg, and Manheim had been rolling it in his fingers a lot lately. He had much to worry about. His Senate subcommittee on private-sector research was moving sluglike through the bureaucratic process, and in a few days he would have to stand before them and convince them that genetic engineering firms needed freedom from the constraints of the Federal Drug Administration—no easy task.

46

Manheim was a firm, outspoken believer in free enterprise who accused the FDA of dragging its feet with drugs that could be manufactured in the United States and serve as viable cures or treatments for people in desperate medical straits. The FDA, stuck in government mud of its own making, was too damned conservative, cautious, and political for his taste.

He was particularly concerned about how the agency's sluggishness hurt his own Florida constituency. The elderly suffered from the lengthy FDA approval process. Many of them were feeble and dying; some were plagued by Alzheimer's disease and desperately needed these new medications. If he was able to get this bill passed, these people might have a chance that they did not have now.

His own mother had died of Alzheimer's disease. Her illness was an agonizingly long ordeal, a disintegration more than a death. He had watched her mind degenerate to a point where she did not know who she was or why she was alive. She did not even know her son anymore. But did the FDA care?

When his daughter Rebecca died of leukemia, the dam had broken. Manheim was not going to wait any longer; there would be no more dragging of feet. Everything had happened to him in a chain reaction. He had fallen to pieces after the death of his mother and his daughter—three weeks apart. The time to sit by and feel sorry for himself was over.

Curt Manheim was not politically naive, but when it came to genetic research, his emotions began to rule. At the same time he knew that the FDA would fight back. If he wanted results, he would have to pilot this measure through.

The bill was critical for another reason. If he could not get it passed—making sure the riders he insisted on got through—the FDA would move as it had never moved before and swoop down on the research and development departments of private companies.

He pushed himself out of the chair and walked to the window to watch the Washington, D.C., dawn. First his mother, then his daughter. Then, when things were at their worst, his wife announced that she had had enough. He knew he had driven her away with his anger, and he did not blame her for leaving. But he could blame the health agencies for their lack of action. And he was going to do something about it.

The view from the Senate Office Building always inspired him. As a boy he had dreamed of standing here and of living in the White House. He had not known then what it would be like to have everything on the line. He could have taken his colleagues' advice and dropped this unpopular crusade, but then, what was holding public office all about if not for taking positions, working for the good of your constituency, promulgating the public good? The closer the time came for a vote the more he realized that this was the most critical moment of his personal and professional life.

He had planned to make a series of speeches in various cities around the nation explaining and defending Americans' right to take successfully tested drugs not necessarily approved by the FDA or the National Institutes of Health. He had built into his proposal strict safeguards that would, by implication, limit the agencies' power. He was asking his colleagues to choose between power and preventive medicine. He could give dozens of examples of the misuse of power by the federal health agencies.

Private firms had to be given some leeway in doing research at their own speed and not according to antiquated time constraints. Things happened more quickly now than they did when the agencies were first established. Research was more sophisticated; more alternative cures were available.

One of the first stops on his speech tour would be in St. Petersburg, where the elderly needed drugs that for years had been on the FDA's waiting list. His friend Bill Walters, the publisher of the *St. Petersburg Herald,* had been urging him to speak on this issue. Walters, a key man in Manheim's election campaign, had to be nurtured. Problems had come up with Bill's influential newspaper, and Manheim was not pleased.

Bill Walters left his Sand Key home, north of St. Petersburg in the Clearwater area, and drove south along Gulf Boulevard. It was early in the morning, and though the world outside the car windows looked serene, Walters was not.

His face was drawn; his hair, which was normally trimmed and parted neatly, was windblown and sticky from the humidity. He had been at the house for a meeting with the members of his newspaper's board of directors, who were unhappy about the first in a series of articles by Pat Heller on current medical testing. While the article was not overtly critical of

U.S. Senator Curt Manheim, it was not exactly laudatory, either. "I'm running a newspaper," he told the board, "not a popularity sheet."

"We want Curt Manheim as our senator for a long time to come," said Sid Cullingham, a land developer and the owner of the Tampa Bay Bombers of the NFL. "We want the man from Tampa to stay put, to do us favors, and to keep our good name at the top of the list. We don't want some jerkwater politician from Naples or Miami or some foreign national taking what is rightfully ours and screwing us at this crucial time in our growth. You hear me, Bill?"

"This first article is based on hard facts and the rest of the series is, too," Walters had told him.

"I don't think you understand," said Cullingham.

"I understand that you're trying to put some muscle on me, Sid, and I don't like it."

"That's tough shit, Bill, because I got loads more pressure where that came from and—"

"Gentlemen, gentlemen," Sally Beaumont, a St. Petersburg Beach condo developer interrupted. "This will get us nowhere." She turned to Walters. "Now, Bill, you know very well that if this first article is an indication of what's to come, we're going to have a lot of difficulty turning the tide back in Senator Manheim's favor. He has an election coming up. He'll be down here soon to speak to the people who elected him by the largest measure ever, and the vote here was just barely enough to swing the rest of the state. All we're trying to do is to protect our own. If you publish articles critical of him, you'll have to expect pressure from us."

The meeting had ended an hour ago, and Bill Walters was still furious. His attempt to bring a big important issue to the public was backfiring in a way he had not expected. His readers were riled up, as he had expected them to be. But this issue with Manheim was something else again. The truth was that he was torn between the public's need to know the facts and what those facts could eventually do to Manheim's career and finally to the area's economy. Where, he wondered, was his allegiance? He felt uncomfortable with what he had read in Pat Heller's piece, but he could not in good conscience back down and make her write the others with a softer angle.

Still, he wrestled with the problem. He wanted to remain true to the spirit of the paper, seeing things as they were and telling the story that way. But with the heat from his high-rolling associates on the board, who had a vested interest in maintaining the coastline's growth and prosperity, he was torn. It all came down to money.

Curt Manheim had beefed up Tampa Bay–St. Pete prosperity. He had promised, and delivered, more revenue, and he had begun several projects. If Manheim lost the November election, those projects would never be completed, and the capital would find its way into other coffers.

When Walters arrived at the *Herald* offices he found a telephone message from Manheim—two of them, in fact. "How'd he sound?" he asked his secretary.

"Fine the first time, not so fine the second."

"All right, we might as well get this over with."

A few moments later the call went through. Walters

took a deep breath, drank some iced coffee, and swung his chair around so that it faced the Gulf of Mexico, where a fishing boat chugged through the channel, heading out to sea.

"Hi, Senator," Bill said.

"Hello, Bill. Guess who just read Pat Heller's article and is not happy."

"You know how these things are. They blow over in no time, and before long people forget all about them."

"Except that this article is the first in a series, Bill. Says so right here in front of me. Why is this woman after me?"

"She's not after you. She has information that points to the fact that a lot of drug manufacturers put pressure on legislators to get products out early. Some of these new drugs have cost lives."

"Look how many lives the drugs have saved!" the senator replied.

Bill laughed uneasily. "You don't have to convince me. I know what's been happening."

"Then why in the hell are you allowing this series to run? You know I'll be down there in a couple of days, and I'll be walking into a nest of vipers."

Bill put his legs up on the windowsill and continued watching the boat. "Look at it this way. You'll have a lot more interested people out there, and you'll give them the ammunition they'll need to vote enthusiastically for you. You'll make them believers."

"You are so full of shit sometimes."

"But so right sometimes, too, old friend."

"I want you to hold off on the series for a while—say, until after the election."

"I can't do that."

"You're the publisher. You can do anything you want."

"If I kill the series, everyone will cry collusion. We'll get more bad press about that than you'll get for your stand. People know about my friendship with you, and the word will be that we talked and I bowed to your pressure. That will make you look like a bad politician and me like a newspaperman in a bad politician's pocket. That alone could cost you the election if the wrong people take up the banner. Don't you see that, Curt?"

Walters could hear Manheim's labored breathing, and knew the senator was rolling his worry egg through his fingers.

Manheim said, "Have the writer use a different slant so that I don't look like such a drug monger. I'm not, you know. The FDA is filled with old men who are afraid to say yes to a new drug for fear of damaging their reputation."

"I can't tell the writer what to do, but I can make suggestions. Believe me when I say that I approved of the series because I thought you would benefit from it, but this reporter of mine—her husband is a doctor, a gynecologist—is smart and canny and has some medical training herself. And, as you can see, she's one hell of an investigator. She dug through a different canal."

"Do what you can, Bill, would you?" Manheim said solemnly.

"I will, and Joan and I will see you for dinner on Saturday?"

"Arrange a meeting for me with Pat Heller so that I can convince her that what I'm doing is from the heart and legitimate."

"It's done. Anything else?"

"Isn't that enough? See you Saturday."

Walters hung up and walked over to the large glass partition dividing his office from the others. This series was not turning out the way he had envisioned. He wondered what else Pat Heller had found. Already the paper had gotten a hundred calls about the article, wanting to know what role Manheim played in allowing dangerous drugs into the marketplace. The callers also wanted to know what other problems the passage of Manheim's bill would create. These were issues that Walters would have to deal with.

What would happen if he pulled back, if he changed the angle of the series so that it would do less damage to the senator's public image? But that alternative brought his own integrity into question. Would he be willing to throw it all up in the air for a friend whose allegiance to him was not quite clear? Was it in the best interest of the public, of the paper, of Bill Walters, to support Curt Manheim on this if, in fact, Curt Manheim was wrong?

One way or another, he would have to get Pat Heller in here to find out what else she knew.

7

"Morning, Miss Adams," Josh said. "How about some mediocre coffee?" He found her in the conference room connecting wires and surrounded by various pieces of new computer equipment.

"No, thanks. I'm almost finished here. Will Dr. Ellison be able to join us for the demonstration?"

"He'll drop in between patients, but to tell you the truth, computers are another planet to him."

She looked tired. Though she wore the green silk suit as if it had been made for her—which it might have been, judging from the way it clung to her body—there were deep worry lines around her eyes. There was also a faint sheen of perspiration on her face. He felt a rush of tenderness for this hardworking young woman.

He waited as she connected a terminal to the laser printer and set the keyboard in place. The equipment looked impressive; the terminal had a wide screen, and the colors—green and gray—melded with the rest of the room. He did not see any brand label on the equipment—Samantha's secret supplier.

"Ready for the demonstration?" she said, standing up.

"Hang on a minute." Josh went into the other room and came back with Julie, who greeted Samantha by raising her coffee mug, no smile, no "good morning." It wasn't like Julie to snub anyone.

During the hour-long demonstration Josh's mind was in a dozen different places. Knowing that Julie, who had a mind like a sponge, would take in every word, Josh spent most of the time worrying about his practice, about Pat and why she was acting more harried lately. He worried that Amy was aware of how tentative things were between her mother and father.

"Oh, no!"

Samantha had apparently made a mistake with some wiring, and the printer started beeping. It sounded worse than it was, she explained, but she seemed to be thrown off balance by the miscue and angry that it had interrupted her sales pitch. She frantically went about reconnecting wires.

"It's okay," Josh said, trying to make her feel better.

"No, it isn't," she said. "This is supposed to work perfectly!"

She saw how they were reacting to her outburst and stood there as if wondering if they wanted her to go on with the pitch. Josh pictured himself with his arms around her, assuring her that no small slip-up could erase the excellent impression she was making.

He smiled at her. "Keep going; you're doing a great job."

She gave him a tentative, grateful smile.

"How's it going, folks?" Jim Ellison's blond head peeked around the corner. "This must be . . . Sam Adams?"

"Samantha," she said, extending her hand.

"Always a greater pleasure to meet a Samantha than a Sam. How's your audience over here?"

"Very supportive." She gave Josh a look that made him blush. "I'll be happy to start over, Dr. Ellison, if you—"

"God, no. You'd be wasting your time. If Josh says go ahead, that's good enough for me."

"Then by all means," Josh said, "go ahead."

"Why don't I put my machine through a short drill?" Samantha proceeded with some complex maneuvers that made no sense to Josh. By the time she had pointed out the equipment's most impressive capabilities, it was clear to Josh that the machine was first rate, and he was glad to leave its operation to Julie.

Samantha turned to Josh. "Are we ready to talk installation?"

"Julie?" he said.

"Go for it."

"I'll have it in and set up by Monday afternoon."

"Monday?" The other companies had said they'd need at least a week and a half.

"I'm afraid that's as soon as I can do it. I have other—"

"No, Monday is good. What do you need from me?"

"For now, just a handshake. Later, a check for six thousand dollars, when you're completely satisfied with the system. I'll bring a service contract and you can read it . . . over lunch tomorrow?"

"I'll look forward to it. How about noon?"

As he shook her hand he looked into her eyes and made a chilling discovery. Now he understood why the computer screen had seemed different to him. Her eyes were the same luminescent green as the characters on the monitor.

When Josh arrived home that night he couldn't find Pat, and there was no sign of dinner cooking. It was just after seven, and when time permitted, they usually ate at seven-thirty. He called out, but there was no response. For a moment he panicked and wondered if something had happened to Amy. He went to the head of the stairs and shouted up to her.

He found Pat in her office in the sun-room surrounded by notebooks and magazines.

"I was calling," he said, surprised by the anger he heard in his voice.

"Hello to you, too," Pat said calmly.

"Why didn't you answer?"

Pat looked up from her writing and glared at him. "I didn't answer because I didn't feel like talking to you. I'm up to my ears in work. I wasn't expecting you home because for the past two weeks you've been on time only once, and I'm not about to jump up to greet you with flowers and soufflés just because you suddenly show up."

"Jesus. What did I do?"

He stood in the doorway, not wanting to stay and argue, but not wanting to leave without a small note of warmth from his wife. He stepped into the room, raising his hands in mock surrender.

"I know apologies don't count," he said, "but things have been hell at work." That sounded trivial. "Deformed births and deaths and dragons at the gate." Pat's glare softened and she pushed her notebook to one side. Josh went over to her and gave her a kiss on the cheek. "Why don't you give that a rest and come out to dinner with me?"

"Amy and I went to Arby's. She's been short on parental contact these days."

"Hey, Pat, come on. I spend a lot of time with Amy. I don't need to defend myself there."

"You never need to defend yourself. You're blameless."

They faced each other. More like squaring off, Josh thought.

"What are you working on?" he said, trying to break the ice.

"I told you about it on Monday. The FDA drug clearance piece. You said you could get some articles for me."

Josh remembered now.

"You haven't even thought about it, have you?"

"You should have left a message with Julie."

"I have to leave a message for my husband with his

receptionist in order to remind him that his wife exists?"

"She's not my receptionist."

"No, she's the wonder woman of the century. I've heard all about her exceptional talents."

"That's not what I meant."

Pat's eyes filled with tears. She felt too tired to fight. She stood and walked over to the bookcase, feigning interest in a medical volume. She had asked for a few simple articles from the hospital library; it would have been so easy for Josh to pick them up. But it was more than the articles; she missed his interest in her work.

"Why don't you say good night to Amy," she said, "we'll talk later."

"Fine," Josh said in agreement. Wasn't there a time, he wondered, when fights were a welcome opportunity to purge worries and to make up later?

After he left, Pat wiped her eyes with her shirtsleeve and stared at the heavy volume in her other hand, *History of Genetics.* She sat down to read.

8

WHAT WOULD HAPPEN IF SHE SKIPPED HER MEETING WITH Senator Manheim? Pat wondered, standing before the mirror in her bedroom. "Don't keep it and see how long you'll be working for the paper," she said out loud to herself. She had already changed her outfit three times and still wasn't satisfied. She wanted just the right combination of casualness and authority.

It was two o'clock, and her appointment with the great man was at four. She had already been down to the kitchen for two small shots of vodka—well, one small and one large—and she realized as she was pouring the big one that she had made the appointment with him for the afternoon so that she could justify those shots. She felt as nervous as a whore in church, borrowing a phrase she had overheard from the lawn man. Her notes were beside her, and she was ready for Manheim, not to crucify him but to praise him . . . and then to crucify him. Something was not kosher about the senator's position on private sector research. She didn't know exactly what troubled her, but her instincts told her to keep at it until she found out.

That brought up another issue, and another excuse for a drink. Josh. Their marriage was, as they say, on the rocks. Nobody deserved twelve years of perfect bliss, but neither was anyone supposed to endure such pain at the thought of throwing it all away. She loved him. And their sex, when they had it, was phenomenal. That in itself had kept a lot of the marriage together. Sex took the edge off, it brought them closer, it made them laugh, and when they did without it for a while it made them crazy. The absence of sex was now making them crazy, and the longer they went without it the worse things got. Neither of them was making a move to get things heated up again. They were like two children in a sandbox fighting over their own territory. And they weren't even trying to talk it through.

She finished the drink and hid the bottle away.

She draped an emerald scarf around her neck and, satisfied with how it accentuated the beige outfit, grabbed her notes and went out the door.

Instead of holding the interview in Bill Walters's office, where she felt she would be compromised, she had suggested the Hilton restaurant on St. Petersburg Beach. The restaurant was perched at the top of the hotel and rotated to offer the best panoramic view of both the city and the Gulf of Mexico. Pat rode the glass cylinder elevator to the top floor.

She fumbled through her notes and panicked when she discovered that she had forgotten to include the article on cell replication. It was too late to go back for it. Let's see, she thought, trying to remember what had been so intriguing about that story. The dark experimentation in the gloomy lab. Yes, that was it. Leave five mad scientists alone for five years, allow them to work unchecked, and watch what they produce. Very Gothic, very dangerous.

When the elevator doors opened she walked into the restaurant and was surprised to see a man who looked like Josh seated with a woman at a window table. The back of his head, the cut of his jacket, the way he held his hand by his jaw as he spoke; it had to be Josh.

Distracted by what she saw, Pat walked along the perimeter of the restaurant. A man stood up from his table and blocked her way.

"Mrs. Heller?" he said.

"What? Yes, I'm Pat. . . . Senator Manheim? Well, how do you do?"

She took his extended hand and let him guide her to her seat. "I thought I saw someone I knew," she said.

"It's a good thing this place is enclosed. Otherwise you would have walked right over the edge."

She felt suddenly embarrassed and stared down at her place setting where she saw a flamingo-colored napkin folded into the pyramid shape that restaurants found so clever.

"Are you all right, Mrs. Heller?"

"Yes, quite. Perhaps I could have some water."

Manheim signaled for the waiter while she went

through her bag for her notes, which she found and placed before her. Every so often she looked up to find Manheim staring at her. He was a handsome man, but a bit too slick for Pat's taste. His teeth, if they were his, were straight and perfectly white. The silver in his hair was so evenly distributed it looked as if it had come out of a bottle. His nails were buffed and manicured, and his tan was spread across his face like butter. Pat wondered if his toes were as well scrubbed. Here before her sat the perfect automaton politician.

After a few moments of chitchat, she looked into his blue eyes and said, "Do you advocate the removal of government restraint on all private sector research and development?"

"Of course not."

"Your bill will surely lead to that, will it not?"

"Not at all."

"What's to prevent your bill from inviting any company to bypass government regulations, or at least challenge them in court, while continuing to research and manufacture whatever it pleases?"

"Current government stopgaps. I have no intention of throwing a wall in front of the FDA."

"What about genetic research?" She watched him carefully on this and saw what she construed as a single flicker of the eyelid, and then he was back.

"What about genetic research?" he said.

"This is a big area. You are on record as having said emphatically that genetic research is the opportunity for mankind to rediscover itself through science. If that's not advocacy, I don't know what is."

Manheim drank some water and dabbed his mouth

with his flamingo-colored napkin. "Mrs. Heller, I am for advancement through scientific inquiry, and genetic research is an important and expanding field of inquiry."

"You have stated that . . ." She checked her notes and read: "Last November twentieth, I quote: 'The United States of America cannot afford to wait for the slow grinding wheels of the government leviathan to speed up to the current world pace. America is falling behind the rest of the world in genetic research.' Have you changed your mind on this issue?"

"I have not."

"How about this: 'Cell replication and genetic cloning are as natural to scientific growth as breathing is to a child.' You said that at the Harvard Medical School last winter."

"I did indeed, and they cheered, because they knew more than the rest of the population, which is not informed. I am trying to educate the public as best I can through these speeches and by getting this bill passed."

"Why are you in such a hurry, Senator Manheim?"

"I am in no more of a hurry than anyone else who is aware of the problem."

"There is another problem that no one but you seems to be aware of, Senator." There, the flicker again. Pat didn't know why she had said that. She'd had no solid reason for making the remark, except to use it as a fishhook, to see what it would catch. It caught him all right. This time there was much more than a single flicker in those baby blue eyes of his.

"What do you mean exactly? What problem?"

Keep fishing, she told herself. "There seems to be something personal involved here, Senator. What is it?"

"I don't know what you're talking about."

"I doubt that." She stared straight at him, wondering where she would take this train of thought. One thing she knew: he was getting nervous. Flicker, flicker, flicker. She glanced down at her notes. "Quote: 'If there is one science that needs our full support—which means government hands off—it's genetic science.' Why be so secretive, Senator? I understand your frustration with the FDA, but you seem more interested in hiding things from them than in working with them."

Manheim smiled at her, showing his perfect teeth. "Why are you angry with me?"

"Angry?" Was she angry, she wondered? "I will tell you this, Senator. I am a DES baby. My mother took prescribed drugs that ended up causing me and tens of thousands of others to be more susceptible to cancer and a number of other diseases. All because of a drug—DES—that was not thoroughly tested. Thalidomide babies are another example. It goes on."

"I am aware of these and have addressed them. What I would like to know at the moment is why you are angry. You've raised your voice and turned this into an inquisition. I'm here voluntarily to answer your questions. Why does it seem that I'm on trial?"

"Because there's something fishy going on here, Senator, that I am going to find out about."

"Mrs. Heller, would you be specific so that I can respond with something concrete?"

She looked at her notes. "I quote: 'We need to get as close to perfection as we can in this random, imperfect world, and genetic research is the path to it.' American Medical Association, Seattle, March of last year. You did say this, yes?"

Manheim pushed himself away from the table and stood, buttoning his jacket. With his middle and index fingers he pinched the knot on his seventy dollar tie. "I am afraid this interview is over, Mrs. Heller. I'll be going now. You obviously don't want to hear what I have to say. Besides, I have an engagement with Bill Walters, whom you know."

"My boss."

"Yes, indeed."

"I am trying to understand your position, Senator, and I am not interested in doing a puff piece. I'll get the rest of the story without you. I hoped you'd be interested enough to have your own views recorded here. Apparently you're not."

"Look, let me tell you something." He aimed a thick finger in her direction. Then apparently he thought better about what he was about to say and lowered his voice. "It would be a grave mistake to go against me on this bill."

"Is that a threat?"

"A simple point of fact. Excuse me and good day."

Pat stayed at the table, fiddling with the napkin. She had blown it with Manheim, but dammit, something lay stinking below the surface. He was not being straight; her instincts told her so. Her instincts also told her to get into the car and either return home or go to the office. She did not obey them and instead ordered a vodka on the rocks and sat watching the gulls swoop down over the beach.

She shivered when she thought about the rage in Manheim's eyes—just a millisecond of fury telling her not to take his threat lightly. The man was dangerous. He could do things. To her. To Amy. To Josh.

"Get rid of her," Manheim said. "She's out to crucify me."

Bill Walters leaned back in his chair. He had never seen Manheim this angry or distracted before. Something was wrong besides the pressure of the election. In the past, Curt Manheim had embraced the challenge of elections and garnered strength from the fight for bill passage. Now he was rigid with anger over a newspaper article. "You're serious?" Walters asked.

"Never more so, Bill. She was not conducting an interview but an indictment." Manheim had been pacing before the window. Now he sat on the edge of the desk and began slapping Walters's lead paperweight methodically into his palm. "She didn't ask me anything significant, nothing pertinent. She told me what she thought and then didn't want to hear my response. Is she out to get me? Why? Because she is a DES baby. That's ancient history. We have come leagues since that time. Furthermore, when she walked into the restaurant she was in such a daze that she barely knew where she was."

"What?"

"She was drunk or flipped out or something. Seriously, I even told her that if it hadn't been for the walls she'd have dropped into the ocean. Is she normally a competent reporter?"

"Excellent. That's why she's on this series. She's written hard-hitting, intelligent pieces in the past and is respected by our medically aware readers."

"Is there trouble at home?" Manheim asked.

"I don't know, but I'll have a talk with her editor."

"More than a talk, okay, Bill?" Manheim stepped away from the desk, cupping his hands around the weight as if in prayer. "I need so much right now. One bad attitude, one wrong turn, could blow it all to hell."

"I'll do what I can, but you know the policy."

"Of course I do, and I also know that yours is one of the fastest-growing, most-respected newspapers in the entire South, receiving well-earned national acclaim. You and I pledged long ago to put the Sun Coast on the map. If I'm defeated and you get a senator from, say, Miami, or even Orlando, you know where their support will be heading. You will have to start building all over again. That would take years, and you might not see significant changes in your lifetime, Bill. On the other hand, if you put a tiny muzzle on this reporter, you might not have to wait. Is that a fair trade-off?"

"I'm listening to you." Walters tried to smile.

"I know you are, old buddy," Manheim said as he let the paperweight drop with a thud onto Walters's desk.

Pat didn't feel well. She was not ill or sick, just upset, nervous. She sat in the kitchen drinking coffee, staring through the window at the darkness, her mind a blank—at least when she wasn't running over the chaotic meeting she'd had with his highness, Curt Manheim. She heard automobile tires crunching the gravel in the driveway. Then the engine went dead, the door opened and shut, and Josh's shoes made more scrunching noises. When he came in, he looked worried and unhappy about something, like a little boy lost.

"What's the matter, honey?" she asked.

"I don't know." He poured himself a glass of juice and sat at the table, staring at the glass.

"More trouble at the hospital?"

He grunted. "At the hospital, at the office, every goddamn where."

"Join the crowd," she said, finishing the coffee and pouring herself another cup.

"Yeah, why's that?"

"Senator Manheim. To think we voted for that man."

"It was him or the Orlando chiseler."

Pat laughed for the first time in days. "Give me a hug."

He reached over and squeezed her shoulders, then planted a light kiss on her mouth. Was it her imagination or did Josh tense when he kissed her? She remembered the couple at lunch, hunkered together.

Josh frowned in that furry-animal way of his and looked across the table at her. "Well, what is it?"

"I'm going on the line tomorrow with Walters, over Manheim and his shady genetics."

"Stay calm. Don't push too hard. You know what

kind of pressure these pols can bring. Say little and keep writing. Meanwhile, I'll try to get some data on these research outfits for you."

"Don't make promises you won't keep."

Josh said nothing. Pat watched him closely, sensing something unfamiliar in his behavior. Or was she imagining things in her skittishness about her afternoon battle scene at the restaurant? "Manheim could be a lot of trouble," she said. "He threatened to come after me if I oppose him on the Senate bill."

"That's the democratic way, isn't it? He's a big blowhard. If it matters, I'm behind you all the way."

"Of course it matters. But . . ."

He looked up quickly, then away. "But . . . ?"

"You want to talk about what's on *your* mind?"

She reached across the table and stroked his cheek, her eyes boring into him, questioning.

"I do love you," he said halfheartedly. With that he got up and plodded over to the refrigerator for another glass of juice.

"I thought I saw you at the Hilton today," she blurted out before she could stop herself.

He turned back from the refrigerator and searched her face for anger or suspicion, but she was gazing at him with the same tenderness of a moment ago. "I was there with a computer rep. We're getting a new system. Why didn't you come over?"

Pat shrugged, a little sadly maybe, but accusingly, too. He went over and held her and whispered that if she hurried, he promised to be awake when she got upstairs. He squeezed her one more time and kissed her favorite spot on the neck and went upstairs.

Alone in the kitchen, Pat cradled her coffee cup in her hands. Something was dreadfully wrong, way out of whack, but there was nothing she could point to. All these instincts, she thought, and nothing to pin them to.

The next morning when she entered the editorial offices of the *St. Petersburg Herald* she was greeted effusively by her editor, Harold Carey. She could not mistake the looks she got from the newsroom staff as she was whisked through. Poor girl, the looks said. Good luck—you'll need it. Kill yourself and get it over with. What was going on?

Bill Walters was in Harold's office when she arrived. He glad-handed her and couldn't say enough about how well she was doing. He told her it had been an honor to work with her over these few short years, and of course he was looking forward to many more great years with Pat on the *Herald* team. She started getting the idea that she was being set up. But for what?

After the long-winded speech, Walters crossed his bony knees and ran a hand through his thinning gray hair.

"Pat," he said, readjusting himself in the chair, "we have a problem here that you can help straighten out."

Here it comes, she thought, whatever it is. "What problem is that, Bill?" She looked quickly to Harold, who lowered his eyes.

"Manheim. We want you to back off the series for the time being."

"Back off?" She didn't think she'd heard him right.

"Yes. Until after the election."

She took a deep breath and let her eyes sweep along the desktop. Keep calm, she told herself silently. Speak slowly, evenly, with no emotion. "Until after the election, when it'll be too late and public interest will have waned? Is that it?" By the time the words were out it was all she could do to hold back, be circumspect. The whole scene, being played out so flagrantly by these two, enraged her.

"No, that's not it," Walters said with irritation.

"What, then?"

"The end. The series is killed. The decision is final."

"Okay, why don't I take it to the *Orlando Sentinel* or the *Miami Herald?* I'm sure they'll be very much interested, as interested as they are in having their candidate win over Manheim. I'll tell them what I have is too hot for the suddenly timid *St. Pete Herald.*"

"Will you please listen to me?" Walters said, his face red.

"Of course, Bill."

As he shifted his position again he looked as if his mind was shifting into another gear. Pat could see the metrics of an idea taking shape.

"We need Manheim on our side," Walters said. "We need him in the U.S. Senate. He feeds and nurtures us, Pat. He feeds and nurtures the Tampa Bay area and the Gulf Coast—the Sun Coast here. If he goes, we take a major step backwards."

Pat was prepared for that. "Why is he pushing so hard for legislation with repercussions extending far beyond the Sun Coast? If his bill gets through, drug and pharmaceutical companies—not to mention laser and genetic firms and who knows what else?—will have free rein to experiment on anything they damn well please. Manheim's Senate bill could mean that an entire slew of unchecked drugs and other products could be manufactured and slipped into the marketplace, creating a new black market. Viruses could start and turn into plagues. We could have a bunch of Dr. Jekylls and Mr. Hydes marching around if the government is taken off the case and free enterprise is allowed to run rampant." She inhaled deeply and pushed forward, afraid that if she gave Walters a second, he would stop her before she'd said what she wanted to say.

"If there are no regulatory measures taken on nuclear warheads or wild cures or genetic engineering, which is at the top of Manheim's list, we could have sanctioned wholesale murder in this country. The facts I've gathered support this, Bill; it would be criminal to turn a blind eye. We need to exercise caution with this, not offer an outright endorsement, which is exactly what the paper will be doing if you kill this story."

Harold leaned forward. His glasses slid down on his long nose, and his hair flopped over his forehead. "Pat, we have to back off for the time being. We're killing the series. Sorry."

"That's a real shame," she said, standing.

"What does that mean?" said Walters, standing with her.

"I'll just have to see." She shrugged. "Regroup and all that."

"I want you off this. It's the end."

"Is that a threat?" she asked from the doorway, sickened at what she was hearing. "Sounds like one to me. First Manheim, now you. What happened to the experienced newspaperman who told me over and over again that he would get to the bottom of any story, no matter what? Who would bury kings if they deserved it? I guess that man has buried himself . . . under pressure from a United States Senator who is up to no good. You are as corrupt as he is, and you are no longer a newspaperman, Bill. Congratulations. You have turned into one more political pimp."

With that she threw open the door and strode out of the office, past the desks and the gaping reporters behind them, past the water cooler gang and the copyboys and into the hot sunlight. She wondered what in the hell she had done and, more important, what she was going to do.

9

THEY WERE SATISFIED WITH A JOB WELL DONE.

The *Fall Springs Gazette,* which had been sent to them from Dr. David Morris's hometown, was spread out over the laboratory table. Two men, one in his mid-forties and the other in his seventies, in white lab coats, were drinking tea and reading an obituary.

The article called Dr. David Morris's death a suicide. Dr. Morris, the paper said, had injected himself with a syringe filled with morphine.

The two men had learned from an accompanying report that no one who knew David intimately, in particular his wife Melanie, could fathom why he had taken his own life. He had been depressed lately, they all admitted, but not enough to kill himself. He had been drinking all afternoon, but on the rare occasions when he had drunk in the past, he had been a good-humored guy.

Yet the evidence was there—the syringe with his

fingerprints on it, plunged into a vein in his left arm. There was no note, which his wife thought was very unlike him, the most meticulously prepared man she knew.

Dr. Ben Brost, his associate at the hospital, admitted to police that Dr. Morris had been concerned recently over the medical complications of several patients.

Despite Mrs. Morris's protestations that her husband was not capable of suicide, the authorities found no evidence to justify any further investigation. The case was closed.

The two men finished their tea, hung up their lab coats for the night, and walked out of the large medical complex. They bade each other good evening and drove home, secure in the knowledge that one more obstacle in their path had been dispatched.

10

Santa Fe, New Mexico

MARIAN POTTER DECIDED THAT THIS WOULD BE HER LAST child. The labor—fifteen hours—and the pain that went along with it were not worth another effort. This was her third child, and no matter how much pressure her husband put on her to have another, she was not going to give in. Enough was enough.

When Dr. Ted Tozian pulled the baby out of her and held it up for her to see, she gasped and began to sob. She could not speak and was just barely able to let out little hysterical grunts. The sight of it! Wisps of pink hair. Tiny sea green eyes. The child looked hideous. She swore it had to be a joke; this was not her baby.

The look on Dr. Tozian's face told her he felt the same thing. This redheaded, green-eyed baby that looked like a cartoon kid had to belong to someone else. Who had this coloring in her family? Nobody! Throw it back, she wanted to shout, and broke into gales of hysterical laughter at the thought.

"I went through a fifteen-hour labor for this!" she managed to say. "Tell me this is a bad dream, Dr. Tozian. Please say it's the drugs or something. I won't take that child. What am I saying? What—"

"It's common, Marian, for an infant to look a little unusual at first," he said. "But soon she'll take on the characteristics and coloring that you expect to see."

It was not her baby. There had to be a mistake. She could not control the stream of tears or the cries. She was deathly afraid of the consequences of allowing her husband to see this baby. If only she could communicate this to Dr. Tozian, but she was losing consciousness and could not get the words out. Then everything went dark.

An hour later she woke to screaming. Male screaming. She recognized her husband's voice.

"Marian, you awake, for chrissake? What the hell's going on here with this kid? Whose is it?"

She wanted him to go away, to let her go back to her nightmares. What was this horrible child she had given birth to?

"Mr. Potter, you'll have to leave," a woman's voice was saying. Marian peeked over the covers to see the nurse and Dr. Tozian trying to calm her husband.

"Why don'tcha tell me now, Marian? Lay it out. You screwed Bill Farrell, didn't you? This is one hell of a way for me to find out. You and Bill, you lying bitch. Red hair. Green eyes. Who else we know with red hair? Bill Farrell. I ain't taking care of his kid, no way! I'm going over to his place right now and shoot the son of a bitch. Won't his wife be interested to know what popped out of you?"

"No, Stan," she said. She could barely hear her own voice, it was so weak. She tried to push herself up, but the pain drove her back down again. "Stan!"

He kept shouting as he was led down the hall and out of sight. Oh, God, she thought, what has happened? She would never have had sex with Bill Farrell. She thought all of this tension was behind her—the weeks of accusations, her husband's terrible jealousy. How could she have had this baby—this red-haired, green-eyed monster? She started thinking crazy thoughts. One time Bill had kissed her and pressed up against her. Could something have gotten through? What other explanation could there be? Oh, Lord, she prayed, what is happening to me? She felt faint again and called for the nurse. Ribbons of pain ran through her, and her head pounded with other kinds of agony. She felt something rise up from her stomach and flow out of her mouth. Where was the doctor? She felt thick-headed and woozy. She called out, but her voice sounded hollow. She couldn't keep her eyes open. Nothing seemed to matter now but the floating feeling that was taking over. She did not fight it. She tried calling for the doctor again, but it didn't matter anymore. There was nothing he could do.

Ted Tozian left his office at Santa Fe Memorial after 10:00 P.M. and drove northwest toward La Jara in the foothills of the Nacimento Mountains. Breathing the desert air was a kind of therapy for him in these terror-filled times. He longed for the days of medical school when his energy was high and he was in love and the future was out there for him. The single blemish on his med school memories was the letter that had arrived last week announcing the death of a classmate, David Morris. When the word came, Ted had sequestered himself for five hours in his library, where he pulled out his medical school yearbook and pored over photos and inscriptions of the men and women to whom he had been so close for all those years.

It had been an exhilarating time for him, filled with fond memories. He looked at the young, eager faces of his classmates—David Morris and Bart Miller, Josh Heller and the others. What a glorious time.

Time gone by. Now everything was shot to hell. The malpractice insurance problems, the overwhelming bad fortune of the past few months. The deaths, the genetic defects, the grotesque babies, the mistakes.

And then there was Sandra and her computer company, not to mention her body, and his soul, which she seemed to have taken along with his check for $6,000. Ted believed that he could never lose control like this, and with a woman he barely knew. He had become an emotional wreck with her. The old joke about crawling across one hundred miles of desert for a woman—no old joke here. He had done it, and more. "Mesmerized" was too soft a word for what he had felt.

He was now a slave to her will. He had been reduced, in two short months, to a blithering idiot in love.

His only respite was the time he spent out here at the cabin in the foothills, listening to the sounds of the desert and thinking—about Sandra, and about Barbara, who had taken the boys to Denver to stay with her mother until good old reliable Ted returned to his senses. But he wasn't returning to his senses. He was losing what few senses he had left.

At the end of the property, where the main highway joined the dirt road that led to the cabin, he stopped the car and got out to check the mailbox and the current in the fences. He kept three saddle horses in the barn and two ponies for the kids. Would they ever ride them again? he wondered.

He walked back to the car and drove the half mile to the cabin. For the last four years he had spent fall weekends making the cabin livable for his family. He had added two bedrooms and a back porch that looked out over the mountains.

He stood on the small patch of lawn in front of the house. The stars were out in their glory, and the distant mountains looked like smooth hibernating animals. How long was he going to be able to appreciate this beauty with so much tension in his life? The land he had always loved now seemed as heartless as a woman primping beside her husband's deathbed.

He thought about the new Christmas baby—his fifth. His partner, Rex Wilkes, had called them that— Christmas babies. Asked why he had chosen that name, Wilkes replied, "Red hair, green eyes. Isn't it obvious?"

Something was very wrong, and Tozian was determined to find out what it was. This many disasters could not be just a matter of bad luck; they had to be man-made. He had questions, and tomorrow morning, when he returned to the hospital, he would take a good hard look around and make sure the questions were answered. And he knew exactly where he would start.

He heard a sound coming from the barn. The horses should have been out grazing on the range. Odd, he thought. They had not come to greet him as they usually did.

He went inside the house for a kel light and took it to the barn, where he pulled the latch and swung the double doors open. He shone the light into the stalls and then down to the other end of the barn where he saw, lined up side by side in a ghostly pack, the three horses and the ponies standing there, five abreast. They seemed frightened, but restrained, as if they were being held back. That was when he noticed the lead ropes around their necks.

He aimed the light behind them and saw a figure.

"Hey," he said to the familiar figure coming out into the open, "what are you doing out here?"

A blinding flash of light was his answer. He reeled back from it before the shock of understanding stopped him. The figure moved in on him. Ted read uncertainty on the intruder's face and wondered what the hell was going on.

"I don't want to," the intruder's familiar voice said, "but I can't help it."

Ted decided to make a run for it.

He heard the sound of ropes being freed, followed by whinnies and hoofbeats. He looked up to see the five horses, released from their leads, bearing down on him. He darted toward the back wall and pressed himself against the boards. The horses reared and kicked, and the first blows glanced off him. He saw a pair of human legs in the background. The intruder was ordering the horses forward. Ted tried to climb the boards, but the horses' heavy bodies lunged into him and knocked him down.

With nowhere to go, he threw his arms over his head and curled his body into a ball.

The first blow came, then another and another until he felt only numbness. He felt his knees being broken, and then there was only pain, blinding horrible pain, and darkness.

11

McLean, Virginia

AT NIGHT, AFTER EVERYONE ELSE HAD GONE HOME, Dr. Bradley Burns roamed the halls of his laboratories, DNA, Inc. He conducted this inspection tour, as he did every night, in order to ensure that everything was in its proper place. The tour took two hours, and violations were treated harshly.

He stopped before the mirror in the reception area, as he did each night at this time, to run a comb through his thick auburn hair and to apply drops to his catlike green eyes.

He saw the lanky figure of Dr. Faubus Leung loping down the corridor toward him. Faubus had begun DNA, Inc., with Brad Burns's father long ago and knew the science of genetics better than Brad ever would. Leung did not, however, know the business end of genetic engineering as Brad did—the buying and selling and dealing with the public.

"Hi, Doc," Brad said to the Chinese man, who bowed silently as he walked out the door. The older man was inspiration and security to him and reminded him of the past and of his father, both of which meant a great deal to Brad.

Brad had made sure that every new piece of technology in the genetics field found its way into the DNA, Inc., laboratories before most scientists had even heard of its existence. Brad was careful about hygiene. He made certain that the maintenance staff kept the labs spotless and that his medical staff scrubbed down everything before leaving for the evening.

The need for order and cleanliness was nothing new. His father had drilled that into him early. In his father's lab, where he had earned a nickel for every dozen beakers he cleaned, he could remember getting a slap across the mouth for each one he left dirty. The old man had taught him well. Build slowly—that was his motto. Patience and persistence count more than the most brilliant flash of insight. Always follow procedure, always take care.

For both father and son genetics had been a way to leap from an unblemished laboratory to unblemished mankind. Brad believed, as his father had, that men were machines created by their genes. If they were to reach their potential, they could not be burdened by imperfections. Like other superlative machines, human beings worked only as well as their parts allowed them to. If its basic components were well crafted, a machine would outperform and outlast all others. Brad explained it to himself as the guarantee of man's survival through flawlessness.

He had personally planted beautiful flowers in the garden of mankind and was now watching their first bloom.

The ringing of the phone interrupted his thoughts. The voice on the other end, which sounded troubled, said, "He's gone."

"Well done, my friend." Burns had heard the tremor in the man's voice. "Something's bothering you. What is it?"

"I never imagined having to do something as drastic as this."

"The sacrifices we make are difficult, I can tell you that. But you must think of your wonderful accomplishment as a challenge you met. You are to be congratulated."

"I didn't know I was this emotionally attached to him."

"Of course you were. That was part of the challenge," said Burns, letting out a satisfied sigh. "Go to bed. In the morning you'll see the glory of your job well done."

Burns ran a freckled hand through his hair. "I have a surprise for you when you come to visit," he said to the caller. "Something I am certain you'll treasure."

He hung up and walked to the picture window that looked out over the dark Virginia landscape. He pulled up a chair, sat down, and put his legs up on the sill.

There was a surprise all right, he thought, frowning, of a most grievous kind. He loathed weak, undisciplined men for the same reasons he feared their rickety, unpredictable nature.

12

It was early evening and the heat hung like syrup in the air. Pat Heller led Amy out of the library, both of them carrying stacks of photocopied research material. They climbed into the car, sweat plastering their clothes against their bodies, and drove home on a highway that was a shimmering blacktopped hell.

In the quiet of the university library, Pat had felt happy to see Amy doing something besides riding horses. Her daughter was becoming an invaluable assistant. Pat could tell that she liked the grown-up feeling the work gave her, and she was already dropping medical terms at the dinner table with confidence.

After the first day of research, in the middle of a poached cod supper, Amy had turned to Josh and said, "Daddy, did you know that some companies right here in Florida are mass-producing interferon from yeast cells?"

"Uh, no," Josh had replied.

"They are," she said with authority, "for the first time ever." Amy looked radiant when Josh gave her a kiss on the forehead and said how grown up and smart she had become.

Pat parked the car in front of the barn, and they carried the research into the house. Josh wasn't home yet, but she found a note saying he was off somewhere and would be back around seven. After Amy went upstairs for a nap, Pat took the research into her study and piled it beside the computer. She poured herself a drink from the vodka bottle she kept hidden in the drawer.

Sitting at the terminal she thought about Manheim's warning. She took another drink and sat in the half light, trying to work through to the source of the problem. How smart could she be, she wondered, pursuing this topic, and involving her daughter as well? Risking herself was one thing, but Amy? "Now that's paranoid," Pat said out loud.

"What's paranoid?" Amy was at the study door, watching Pat go into one of her trances, as she called them. Pat put the vodka down, knowing by Amy's expression that she disapproved of her drinking.

"Paranoia," Pat said quickly, "is when people have delusions of persecution."

"I know what it means," Amy said, "I just couldn't figure out what *you* were talking about." With another furtive glance at the vodka bottle, Amy turned and left the room.

Pat sighed with regret. She knew Amy wasn't blind to the problems she and Josh were having. Children always knew more than you thought they knew, or wanted them to know. But was it fair that Amy adored Josh and only tolerated her? If she knew so much, couldn't she figure out that it was she who had given up the most to raise her and care for her? She knew she had better give up this neglected-wife-and-mother routine, a favorite indulgence of hers for some time now.

Pat peeked around the corner to make sure Amy was out of sight, then poured herself a small vodka before giong back to the research. Right away the familiar prickle of excitement grabbed her; she felt like an intruder sneaking into new and forbidden territory. Before her were hundreds of pages on the science of genetics. Scientists had been meddling in genetics since the nineteenth century, when a monk named Gregor Mendel discovered that there were laws of heredity that predetermined how color and size were passed from one generation to the next. Now farmers were able to crossbreed plants and livestock, and predict their outcome, establishing control over nature. Modern agriculture was born.

The next logical step was delving into man's genetic makeup. Every human cell was a blueprint for the genetic makeup of the entire body. One tiny cell carried enough information to create an entire human being, and in each cell there were over 100,000 genes. Scientists were now just beginning to identify them.

Most of the new genetics engineering firms she read about were using a technique called gene splicing to create medical products like interferon and insulin. Natural interferon, a drug that could act against breast and lymph node cancer, cost $150 per injection. The synthetic product, if it passed federal regulations, would cost a dollar a shot. Hard to argue with that, Pat thought. So why was the FDA holding it up? Why, also, was it restricting Cellform, the company that made several types of interferon and something called hybridomas, pure antibodies that fought against disease.

She kept reading. The biology journals overflowed with glowing reports of advances made in potential life-saving drugs. Pat thought about Faust and the ethical questions about manipulating the natural genetic structure. All these articles were abstract and described techniques not fully developed. Many commented on U.S. Food and Drug Administration sluggishness and complained that miracle drugs faced too many years of testing.

She started to wonder why she had committed herself to such an elusive story. Had her pride been talking when she stood up to Bill Walters? Where was her good sense? Maybe it was no more than a gut instinct, but she knew there was a story here somewhere. Walters would not have taken the series away from her so abruptly without pressure from Manheim.

Manheim. In her frenzy to learn the history of genetics, Pat had lost sight of the original fire, the source of her inspiration. After the disastrous lunch meeting, it was clear to Pat that Manheim had lobbied strongly for government to keep its hands off genetics research. But so did a lot of politicians. With the big genetics firms' potential for earning millions, state leaders wanted this revenue for their constituencies.

Pat knew there was more to Manheim's stand than political posturing. He not only lobbied for it, he insisted, demanded, mandated! And Walters had killed the series. Manheim's anger at her was one thing, but why would he swing his weight so far as to ax the project? She reminded herself that she could not prove anything, not yet anyway, and wondered if Bill Walters would talk to her about it.

The front door banging open and shut snapped her to attention. Josh stood there with his arms folded, scowling. He was staring at the vodka bottle, the piles of paper on the table, the mess. "Again?"

"What do you mean?" she said. "I've been working hard . . ." Her voice trailed off. She knew she wasn't drunk; she'd been too interested in the research, but Josh wouldn't believe her. All he needed as evidence was the bottle and the absence of dinner—imagine, forgetting dinner.

He turned and left the room. By the time she made it out to the kitchen he was already at the refrigerator, fishing around for salad greens. "I can do that," she said, taking the lettuce from him. "I've got fish steaks marinating." Luckily she had doused the fish with soy sauce and sherry before the library trip. "If you start the grill, we can still eat by eight."

Josh gave her a harsh look and headed out to the patio. She could hear him dumping charcoal onto the grill and pouring lighter fluid. A few minutes later she was out on the patio with him. He looked ragged and tired. In the firelight, his face was puffy from too little sleep. His eyes had a distant look as he gazed into the flames. She wanted to put her arms around him, even if only as a gesture of friendship.

"Damm it." He kicked the grill and poked the embers with a stick. Then he poured more fluid on the coal, letting the can hang dangerously over the new licks. He looked up, saw her watching, and stiffened. "What is it?" he said wearily.

"What would you like," she said, "vinaigrette dressing or blue cheese?"

"Either one." He shrugged and went back to poking the fire.

She came down off the steps to stand beside him and rub his back. "I'm sorry," she said.

"About what?"

She'd meant it as a general I'm-sorry, and his question threw her. "Just for . . ."

"For being drunk during most of your waking hours. Don't be sorry, Pat. Just stop."

She could feel anger rising up like heat on her skin. "As if you're so perfect," she said.

"We're not talking about me."

"Maybe we ought to!"

Josh looked across at the neighbors' yard. "Maybe we ought to keep it down."

She walked over to the picnic table and sat down, crossing her legs. "That's good. Criticize me. I try to explain, and you want me to shut up."

"Did you listen to what you just said?"

"Tell me, why don't you? You're so goddamn smart."

"Pat, please . . ."

"If you were half as concerned about our goddamn marriage as you are about the neighbors, we'd have a chance."

He laid the stick on the sideboard beside the grill and dropped his head. "Let's not argue."

"Perfect! Get me all pissed off, then back out. Perfect, Josh honey. Fine!" She got up too fast, and her head swam. She reached back to brace herself against the table, and it gave a little, causing her to lose her balance. "We have got to get this thing repaired! How many times have you promised to fix this table?" She was losing it; all she needed was a little drink, something to help her get her bearings. "If you want to continue this I'll be slaving away in the kitchen."

She started for the door and was suddenly stopped by a vision from above—Amy, standing in an open second-floor window, a sad expression on her small face. The look made Pat want to cry, but instead she managed a smile. She lowered her head and ducked inside to the study, where she poured herself half a glass of vodka, which she drank in a single gulp.

A shiver ran through her body as she sat hunched over the small screen. The hangover was not unlike the ones she'd had yesterday and the day before, but the depression that went with it was deeper. It was noon and she had already been in the basement of the library for three hours. She had slipped out of the house, taking Amy to the school bus with her, before Josh got up.

Josh had slept in the guest room again. That made three nights this week. How many the week before? Another few drinks, another fight. Another cold night.

She looked over at the only other occupied desk in the room, where a mousy-looking young woman in a drab, faded dress, her hair tied in a bun at the nape of her neck, sat over her computer. The woman had been there for a couple of hours, and Pat was amazed at her steady concentration. Only the young could do that. When Pat was a student, she could study for twelve hours straight without a break. Those days were gone.

Careful not to disturb the girl, Pat turned on her recorder and spoke into it. "With ten pages of Manheim's personal history I have nothing earth-shattering. Looked at political speeches, platform changes. Voting patterns established, voting patterns broken. His record on medical issues, ten years back. Check to see who his big-money backers are. Are there any in the pharmaceutical business—other doctors, laboratories, and so forth?"

She had been through old newspaper clippings—tedious work, but the only sure way to find the obscure detail that would open the dam. As a U.S. senator, Manheim got his share of attention from the press. Pat was already sick of reading about his journey from riches to more riches.

Tampa land developer inherits millions from family orange groves second in size only to Minute Maid's in the state of Florida. Looking ahead to a political career, he sells the groves to avoid criticism for employing migrant workers at slave wages. He wins a congressional seat, serves six years, runs for the

Senate, and wins. A human rights advocate, but on most issues a staunch Republican. One exception: he opposed strict federal regulations on medical research, with an emphasis on the genetics industry. Why?

She checked her notebook for quotes, dates, and odd facts. After five days she had filled two notebooks, and now she was running into dead ends. Nothing new, nothing remarkable. Nothing, she finally admitted, very interesting. The man was a saint. But she still had an inkling of something unsavory.

She kept at it. She almost missed the headline in Section B of the *Miami Herald:*" State Senator's Mother Dies of Alzheimer's Disease." The paper was dated two weeks after the election. Manheim's mother had kept her illness secret because he was up for reelection. "Her greatest wish," the article read, "was that her son be elected again so that he could help the elderly."

The picture accompanying the story showed a much younger Manheim, holding the hand of a child. "The Senator with his daughter Rebecca," the caption read.

Daughter? Pat could not remember any mention of a daughter in the articles she had read. Rebecca Manheim. Pat entered her name in the computer. She found mention of her in some of the smaller papers. There were no photos or "people" notes. She studied the dates, figuring that Rebecca would have been eight or nine when her grandmother died—that would make her eighteen now. Just the right age for a Florida deb.

Pat checked the society pages but found no mention

of a coming-out party for Rebecca Manheim. She should have at least attended the annual balls, but there was no listing anywhere. Odd. She checked the dates again and landed on the day of her death. With a shudder, Pat called up the February entry and stared at the obituary in front of her: "Senator's Daughter Dies of Leukemia."

"A daughter died. Rebecca. Leukemia," she whispered into the recorder, "three weeks after her grandmother. He lost his mother and his daughter at the same time."

Pat left her things in the library and went outside for some air. The midday sun was a shock after the cold basement. She walked across the street to the beach and took off her shoes. Manheim had been born wealthy; he had become a brilliant businessman and a political leader with tremendous vision and discipline. Pat remembered reading that his marriage had ended in divorce right around the time of the deaths. She made a mental note to recheck that.

What would it be like to lose both a mother and a daughter in a few weeks' time, both to incurable diseases? Would it make a man want to battle against the disease, to erase the plague? Yet she had checked his record of donations. He gave a yearly stipend to the American Cancer Foundation. He hosted dinners whose proceeds went to a children's hospital. A good show, Pat thought, but not exactly the kind of support you'd expect from a man with his financial history. He had no record of supporting cancer research and had not lobbied for any of the new cancer drugs.

Maybe he was afraid of it. Illnesses that killed two

of the most important people in his life were a powerful opponent. Still, with the money he got from the grove sales he could have built a hospital wing or a university research lab. Just a few charity dinners, a couple of personal donations? It didn't add up.

Pat looked out to the ocean and wondered what he had done with all that money? Imagine having that sort of cash, enough to buy anything you wanted. A new tape recorder, a laser printer, a racehorse for Amy, a Maserati for Josh. Pat laughed, singing out, "These are a few of my favorite things." What were Manheim's favorite things? She stopped suddenly; she was definitely on to something here. One thing was for sure: his money was not in cancer wards. She started back to the library.

She gathered her notes and left the dreary basement, intending to find a phone and call her friend Kit Singleton, the paper's financial editor. She was already out in the parking lot when she remembered her tape recorder and went back for it. It wasn't under the notebooks where she had left it, or under the desk. The girl! She was gone. A good tape recorder, left unattended. That was a brilliant move. And her taped notes were also gone.

Why would anyone have taken the recorder and left her expensive Cross pen sitting right on the table next to her pocket calculator? Just the recorder . . . and the tape. She ripped open her briefcase. Her notes were gone, too.

She sat down in the chair facing the computer terminal and remembered Manheim's threat.

13

AT CERTAIN TIMES DURING HIS CAREER JOSH HELLER wished he had chosen a different occupation. He wondered if he had wasted his time on medicine when he could have applied his abilities to writing, painting, or maybe the stage. He liked to think, at times like these when he questioned his choice of professions, that inside him there was a deep love of humanity. He was committed to its comfort and the prolongation of life; he wanted to ease people's suffering. But the older he got, and the deeper he journeyed into medicine, the more uncertain this humane responsibility became for him.

With his ability to reason, to memorize, to conceptualize, he might have served humanity far better, he told himself, if he had become a writer or a teacher, a painter or a playwright. Perhaps it was a fundamental mistake to have believed his mentors when they told him that a doctor's duty was to serve humanity's needs. The ophthalmologist kept the eyes alive, but the poet traveled through the eyes to discover something profound and meaningful deep in the soul. Which was more satisfying, he wondered, preserving life like a doctor or comprehending it like a poet?

Josh popped open a can of beer and listened to the hum of the air conditioner. The shades were drawn, blocking out the glare. Peace. A golf match was on TV, being played someplace up north. Greg Norman poked a two-hundred-eighty-yard drive, was on in two, and two putted for a par. Josh loved to watch golf; it was a game to doze by. He considered it the most difficult sport to master, and yet it looked so easy to play—like life itself.

He slid the hassock over in front of the chair and propped his feet up on it. This seclusion was a real treat for him; he almost never had the house to himself. And now, suddenly, just when he was looking forward to lounging around for a couple of carefree hours, that old enemy, thought, crept in.

Thought number one: He felt guilty sitting here like a slug while Pat was working like mad at the library.

Thought number two: He was vaguely annoyed at her for being gone most of the day when they could have snuggled up together all afternoon. Made a little love, taken a little nap.

Thought number three: He felt terrible for having snapped at her about the drinking last night and then being a jerk and sleeping in the guest room.

Thought number four: It was time to get another beer.

He kicked his feet off the hassock and took the

empty can with him into the kitchen. By the time he got to the fridge he had started to badger himself about being a lousy husband and father, with a wife who didn't love him, a daughter who loved her mother more than her father, and a medical practice on the skids. He was getting a migraine thinking about all this. And now he was on his second beer in ten minutes, after accusing Pat of drinking too much.

He spotted a plate of something wrapped in foil, with a note taped to it: "Sorry about last night. I'll probably miss lunch, so I left you a bite. Love, Pat."

He tore off the wrapping and found a roast beef and Bibb lettuce salad hemmed in by a border of bright green asparagus. Just like Pat to make amends with a flurry of bright colors after an ugly fight. He felt a wave of affection for her.

He popped the second beer and carried the food with him back into the living room. When Pat came home, he would ask her about the Manheim story and insist on reading her research. If he could get Amy a sitter, they might even be able to go out to dinner. The thought of a quiet dinner date with his wife made him happy for the first time in days.

Just as he settled in, and Curtis Strange sent a shot over the trees to within four feet of the pin, the phone rang. He wanted to let it ring without answering, but his conscience told him it might be the hospital.

"What is it?" he snapped into the phone more abruptly than he'd planned.

"I'm sorry. Have I phoned at a bad time?" The voice coming through the line was soft and concerned. "I'll call back later."

"No, no, that's okay." Josh knew who it was right away.

Samantha Adams said, "I'm sorry to cut into your Saturday, but I've been working on some program changes."

"No bother," he said. "If you're going to spend your day working, the least I can do is hear what you've got. Let me get something to write with." He put down the phone and went into the kitchen for a pen and paper. Suddenly he wasn't tired anymore. Back in the living room, he said, "Sorry to keep you waiting."

"You dropped the phone before I could stop you," Samantha said. "I was going to ask you if you would rather meet and go over the program in person. It's a bit involved."

"Yes, of course," he said. "It's just that I hadn't planned on working today. Could we do it on Monday?"

"You must think I'm an idiot," Samantha, said, laughing. "Didn't I tell you I'll be gone most of next week? I've got some business in Chicago."

Had she told him that? The past week had been so frantic that he couldn't remember.

"In that case," Josh said, "if you think it's important, let's get together. Should we meet at my office?"

"Josh, I know this is a big imposition," she said, "but I've got a flight out tonight. I was hoping you would come by my place instead. It's closer than the office, just a few minutes away."

Josh knew that the only way to avoid spending the whole day at his office was not to go in at all. "No problem. I don't like the idea of facing the office today anyway."

"Let me give you directions."

The drive to Samantha's house ran along Tampa Bay. Ships under full sail were bent before the wind, cruising through the choppy waters. A stream of cars raced over the Bay bridge, connecting Tampa with St. Petersburg. Sea gulls glided overhead while deep-billed pelicans stood like Neptune's gargoyles on the bridge searching the water for fish.

Josh was not surprised that Samantha lived in Tulip Beach, an elegant, low-key part of Tampa. Bungalows with very high price tags stood beside the water, surrounded by a golf course, tennis courts, and guard posts. As nice as this section was, Josh wondered why Samantha would choose to live in this isolation when most people her age lived closer to the city. But Samantha Adams was no ordinary young woman. He tried to picture her meeting friends for drinks at some hot club in town, but she seemed too serious for that.

Josh checked himself in the rearview mirror; he looked pale and tired and in need of a week in the islands. He had thought about changing into a shirt and tie but had decided that what he had on—a rumpled blue work shirt and old chinos—felt exactly right for a lazy Saturday afternoon.

He took the exit for Seaview Road and began looking for numbers. Some of the homes were sleek and low, others broad and towering, all of them growing in breadth and girth the farther from the road and the closer to the water he got. Finally he found her number on a large waterfront ranch house with a circular drive and a flamingo-colored guest house.

"Josh, hi!" Samantha waved to him from the doorway. She looked breathtaking in a short azure dress.

"Some place," he said, walking up the drive to greet her. She led him inside through an elegant living room and out to a sun-room filled with flowering plants and Scandinavian furniture.

"I got lucky," Samantha explained. "Friends own this place and leased it to me for the year."

"The year?" Josh said. "What if you need to stay here longer? That is, what if your work's not finished?"

"Not a problem. I can stay as long as I like."

He sat down on the couch where he found some notebooks.

"You may want to look at these for a few moments," she said. "I'll bring us some lunch—that is, if you haven't eaten."

Josh shook his head, remembering the lunch Pat had prepared for him at home.

He watched her float off toward the kitchen. The place was dreamlike, almost Mediterranean with its soft breeze and billowing draperies and the Italian Renaissance music.

Like any good schoolboy, Josh read the notes she'd left for him. Samantha had outlined a plan for linking his office computer up to the hospital lab. As far as he could make out, this would allow him to get test results in half the time. There were nearly fifty typewritten pages—when did she have the time? he wondered—filled with technical symbols and computer program notes that mystified him.

"That's the boring part," Samantha said, coming back into the room. "You just need to worry about the basic idea." She set down a tray of lobster salad, warm rolls, fresh berries, and chilled white wine.

"The basic idea is a good one," Josh assured her. "You amaze me. Everything you do," he said, indicating the lunch as well as the report, "is perfect."

"Now, there's a compliment." Samantha sat down beside him, surrounding him with her fragrance.

Samantha ate while she explained more about the program.

"It's been tried in some smaller offices with great success," she said. "You'll need the cooperation of the hospital lab, but as it saves them time and paperwork, there's no reason why they shouldn't be happy to help."

"So the lab workers enter the test results directly onto a computer?" Josh said.

"Right. A computer linked to the one in your office. All you have to do is press a command code to see if the results are in."

"Which means no more delays in transit, no more botched results. Julie will be ecstatic."

"You'll be the envy of every doctor in the area. Now," she said, "how about a swim?"

No good doctor would let a patient swim so soon after a meal, Josh thought to himself, but he decided to give himself permission to see Samantha in a bathing suit.

She pointed through the glass door to a cabana on the other side of the pool. Inside the cabana he found men's and women's bathing suits, robes, towels, goggles, and thongs. The tiny orange spandex men's suits were definitely not his style, so he pulled on a pair of conventional blue trunks and threw a terry-cloth robe over his shoulders. On the way out he grabbed a pair of goggles; if Samantha swam as well as she did everything else, he had a workout ahead of him.

He found her reclining on a chaise longue in one of the briefest bikinis he'd ever seen. Not a suit to swim in, the strapless top barely concealed her nipples. The smile she gave him was definitely not work-related. He felt too confused to be excited. There she was, fawning and flirting, as though a switch had been thrown and Samantha the serious had become Samantha the seductress.

"I love the sun," she said, stretching out. "It feels so good to be hot before going in for a swim."

Was she joking? He had a hard time reconciling this woman with the computer drone he had gotten to know at the office.

"Is it too warm for you?" she said, fishing in a straw bag and pulling out a tube of sunscreen, then rubbing it over her legs and stomach. There was not a crease or blemish on her porcelainlike skin. She handed the tube to Josh.

"No, I'll go the natural route," he said.

She got off the chaise and stood. Josh noticed that her hair, now loose, hung down to the small of her back. "I'm going in," she said and walked to the diving board, where she executed a very nice jackknife, after which she swam a couple of energetic laps. Josh stepped out of his robe and into the water, then paddled toward the shallow end.

He crawled along through the cool water for a lap or two as Samantha's strong strokes sent rolling wakes against him.

"There are over a hundred species of plants around this pool alone," she said, floating over to him. "I wish I knew their names." She was now close enough so that he could smell the sweetness of her breath.

He laughed nervously. "You mean there's something you don't know? I'm amazed."

She took his arm and said softly, "I don't know everything, not about you."

He didn't like the fact that her body was this close and this naked. "On the contrary," he said, "you seem to know a great deal about me. About my family, my practice . . ."

"I'm talking about what you feel, not your history. What do you feel now?"

He shut his eyes, feeling faint. When he opened them again she was watching him with a feline curiosity. She placed her hands on his shoulders and pressed herself against him. He wanted to reach out for her, but he couldn't. This was not right. "Look," he said, "we're going in the wrong direction here."

"Oh, I don't think so," she said, her lips on his neck.

"You don't, but I do, and it takes two of us to make this happen." He pushed her away and reached back to get a grip on the side of the pool. "I'm sorry, Samantha, but let's not make things too complicated, okay? If I weren't married and things were different . . ."

He hoisted himself out of the water and staggered over to the table for a towel. He felt relatively safe now—embarrassed by this whole thing but relieved.

Samantha stayed in the pool, her face expressionless. "It's late," he said, drying off. "I should be getting back."

Samantha smiled at him. "I'm going to do a few more laps while you change."

He made his way toward the cabana, where he dressed quickly, anxious to get home. He sat on the bench in the cabana and felt like an old man suddenly caught between his desire for this strikingly beautiful woman and his allegiance to his family. On the surface it would have been easy to rationalize a little sex in the pool. He was having trouble with Pat; she was drinking too much. The marriage was shaky. There had been no sex in a couple of weeks at least, maybe longer. It was not easy to ignore the yearnings he felt for Samantha, but who was he kidding?

Samantha was waiting for him by the sliding glass doors.

"It's too bad you have to go."

"I have things to do at home."

"Of course." There was no trace of annoyance or regret in her voice.

"Thanks for the lunch. And the program, of course. You did a lot of work."

Samantha led him through the living room to the front door, where she turned to face him. "It will be a tremendous boon if I can get this program going," she said. "We'll have to spend some time together, but I can promise you that there won't be a repeat of what happened in the pool."

"Thank you."

She leaned forward, and he felt her lips soft against his skin. "I care for you a great deal."

"Right," he said. "Be seeing you, Samantha."

"Good-bye, Josh."

By the time he climbed behind the wheel and looked back at the house, she was gone.

Pat Heller was not in the library, as she had told her husband she would be. Instead, she was in Josh's office with Dr. Jim Ellison, who was examining her. Her regular gynecologist was somewhere in France for a month, and she didn't know anyone else who could perform the examination quickly and confidentially.

Pat had been feeling odd lately, and the symptoms were not unfamiliar to her. When she had been pregnant with Amy she had experienced the same occasional nausea and depression, the sweats and the irritation.

"I know I don't have to keep asking you, Jim," she said to him, "but please don't tell Josh about this."

"What? I didn't tell you? He'll be here in"—he checked his watch—"about five minutes."

"That isn't funny."

Pat was on the examination table, her legs in stirrups. She trusted Jim and knew from Josh and Julie and some of her friends who were his patients that he was thorough and very easy to be with. And he had a sick sense of humor.

"Ow," she exclaimed, "what's that?"

"Part of the examination, dear."

He had pinched her with something and was now putting whatever he had taken from her on a glass slide, which he placed in a cylinder.

"I don't remember that part," she said.

"Uh-huh. It's only been how many years since you were tested for pregnancy? Medicine has progressed just a little since then, but look, I'll tell them not to go forward with anything until they've checked with you first."

"You are the one today, Jim."

"And you, my dear, I believe, are the two today."

She felt the tug. "The two?"

"Congratulations? I use the question mark because I'm not sure you were expecting that answer, but, yes, you are pregnant."

"Oh, my God." She dropped her head back on the table and stared at the ceiling. Pregnant? Now?

She said, "This may not be the best time."

"You weren't taking precautions."

"I was, but I had an infection, and John Billingsley took me off the pill for a month, and there were a couple of nights there with Josh . . ." Her voice trailed off as she thought about those nights not long ago when she and Josh had gone after each other like animals.

"Hello?"

She broke out of the memory and looked at Jim.

"The answer is yes, I stopped taking precautions, and that's obviously when it happened."

"What do you want to do?" Jim sat back and ran his long, slender fingers through the strands of blond hair that had fallen over his face. He was so handsome, she thought, and wondered why some woman hadn't gotten him. A couple of her married friends would not have minded an affair with him, but he gave no one any encouragement in that direction.

She took a deep breath, thinking about what having another child would mean. "Josh and I have been having trouble, Jim. I know a lot of it has to do with the stress around here, but I don't see any letup and neither does he. So having another child at this point . . . I just don't know. Basically, I think I'm in shock at the news."

"There are alternatives," he said, "and you're not that far along."

"May I have a drink?"

"Look, the baby's not old enough to drive yet, so maybe you had better take it easy."

Jim helped her to her feet. "Call me here or at home anytime—to talk, to chat, whatever, all right?"

Outside in the parking lot, Pat leaned against her car door and dropped her head. As if there weren't enough complications, she thought. She didn't know what to do; it was like a bad dream. And yet, way down deep inside she felt absolute joy.

14

KAREN WILLIAMS WATCHED THE CLOCK FROM THE BATH-
tub. Above her a tiny window let in a stream of yellow
light from the street lamp outside, through the potted
geraniums she had placed on the sill. She had been
resting in a tub of warm water for the last hour; it was
now almost 4:00 A.M., and the pain had subsided a
little.

She climbed out of the tub and toweled off, drying
her swollen stomach with special care, as if her child
could feel the gentle rubbing. She felt her baby deep
inside her with painful, tearing kicks. Her baby was
already two weeks overdue. Everything she had read
said that labor should have started by now. She made
her way into the bedroom and bundled herself
beneath blankets and comforters. Another four
hours and finally she could head for Dr. Heller's
office.

Her mother would have told her to go to the hospital emergency room, but she was afraid of hospitals and despite what she had read in the books, she was pretty sure that the pain she was having was normal enough. It was her pain, after all, and she should know.

She had heard somewhere that first pregnancies were hard, especially on nineteen-year-old unwed mothers. She would have felt a lot better if someone had been with her now—a husband, a lover, or even a boyfriend. Except that she wasn't sure who the father was, and none of the guys she dated had been willing to claim the child. In fact, they didn't want to see her anymore after they found out about the baby.

Well, she didn't need them, and her baby didn't, either, not with that attitude.

She used to have a lot of friends she went out with every night. Not that she was any wilder than most of her friends from Tampa. The St. Pete beach kids were different. They were trouble.

She had slept with only three men in her life, unfortunately all at about the same time. She didn't wonder that none of the guys wanted anything to do with her, but she had been hurt and surprised when her girlfriends dropped her as well. It was as if they saw her as a living symbol of what might happen to them, and none of them could deal with that. She knew she'd ruin their fun if she went out with them. Anyway, she was so sick all the time that she didn't want to do anything but lie in bed. This morning, she promised herself, she would go in and tell Dr. Heller about every symptom. She was sure he could do something to stop the pain.

Josh had not been able to get Saturday afternoon out of his head. He had raced home filled with anxiety and guilt only to find a message from Pat saying she had dropped Amy somewhere and gone back to the library.

He pulled into the hospital parking lot and saw an old blue VW in his parking space. To make matters worse, the rest of the lot was full. He felt like ramming the son of a bitch. Instead, he ripped a page out of the notebook he carried in the visor and wrote down the plate number.

He parked on the lawn and started for the entrance. On the way he passed the VW. Inside he saw a young girl slumped over against the car door. He reached through the open window and took her wrist, feeling for a pulse. It was rapid, and she had a fever, but her breathing was regular. He opened the car door and lifted her into his arms. He gagged at the smell of something and then saw the yellow vomit on the seat beside her. The girl opened her eyes and mumbled something about being lonely.

Another car pulled alongside. It belonged to Julie Palmer, who recognized the girl in Josh's arms. She helped him get Karen Williams through the door and into one of the examination rooms, where Josh placed her on a table.

"Undress her and get her ready," he said. Then he noticed the damp circles around the girl's nipples. Julie unbuttoned the patient's shirt and gasped.

115

Karen's breasts were covered with a light green milky substance.

"What in the world!" Julie cried.

"I've never seen anything like that," Josh said.

"What is it?" Karen whimpered.

"Don't worry," Josh assured her. "We need to do some tests. Have you been having any unusual pains lately?"

Karen Williams burst into tears.

Josh performed a pelvic examination on Karen Williams. He took longer than usual, not liking what he saw. When he was finished, he joined Julie in the hall. "She's up to eight centimeters, but the head is still too high. The baby is face up instead of face down." That meant it was stuck, calling for a C-section or maybe a forceps delivery. The ultrasound would tell him what he had to do.

He sat tapping a pencil against the desk top, waiting for the lab results. The phone rang, and he grabbed it on the first ring. He repeated the doctor's words, "Posterior with a hyperextended neck. Figures."

He spent the next two hours pacing and checking the monitor readings. A nurse stuck her head out of the labor room. "Better take a look at this."

The paper strip said it all: the last four contractions showed deep heart decelerations to 100, lasting ten to fifteen seconds after the contractions had ended. The readings indicated a loss of oxygen to the baby's brain, either from cord compression, placental inefficiency, or pressure on the brain itself.

Ten minutes later the decelerations were deeper and longer.

Josh hurried down the corridor into the labor room. "Give me a glove. I want to check her." A minute later she was fully dilated. "We'll go with a forceps rotation. Take her to Delivery and set her up. I'll give her a spinal anesthetic."

On the delivery table they got Karen into a sitting position, bent over, arching her back. Josh painted her lower back with Betadine.

Holding the small syringe, he inserted the long spinal needle between the lower lumbar vertebrae. When he felt the needle penetrate the membrane, he injected the anesthetic. "Okay, lay her flat, put her in the stirrups, and prep her."

He took Kielland forceps from the cabinet for the rotation and grabbed curved Leukardts for the long hard pull and delivery. He scrubbed, put on the sterile gown and gloves, and applied the drapes. Karen's blood pressure was okay, but the fetal monitor showed the baseline heart rate dropping; it was now at 120.

He applied the right Kielland to the head, but it was too high in the pelvis. The left was more difficult, and tighter. He finally got them locked and began to rotate them slowly to the right.

Nothing happened. He applied force, rotating in the opposite direction. Nothing again. What was going on here? Josh could not go harder because of the damage he might do to the vagina, the bladder, or the rectum. A trickle of sweat dripped down his forehead. "Come on, kiddo," he muttered. "Let's have a little help here."

Finally there was a sudden release of pressure and the head turned. He removed the forceps and got ready to use the delivery instruments. Then the head promptly returned to its original position.

After another few tries he managed to get the head turned enough to slip the Leukardts in place. He began the long pull through Karen's pelvic canal. The trick was to use steady pressure for a few minutes, with rest stops for the baby and himself.

This step went smoothly for the first few minutes; then the fetal heart rate dropped to 80, then 70. Time was now crucial. He was losing the battle, but he couldn't turn back. The heart rate dropped again.

He cut a deep episiotomy between Karen's vagina and rectum and applied hard pressure on the baby's head. It was working, but then everything stopped and the head would not budge. He felt around with a finger and found the umbilical cord wrapped tightly around the baby's neck. Heart rate had dropped to 60 and was falling.

With two Kellys he tried to clamp the cord loop but failed and tried again. There was no movement until suddenly the shoulders started out. He quickly suctioned the nose and throat and hollered, "Get the pediatrician on call—*stat!*"

He took a look at the baby and stepped back. It had pale blue-green eyes and a full head of fiery red hair. Its skin was bright blue, and it was not breathing. The nurse looked up for the first time and gasped. She quickly realized how her cry must have sounded and turned away in embarrassment.

Josh grabbed an oxygen mask and placed it over the baby's mouth. Only two vital functions were performing. He knew he should have done a C-section.

The pediatrician, Dr. Birdsall, arrived, took one look at the baby, and recoiled. "I'll be down to the nursery in a few minutes," Josh said to him, and Birdsall carried Karen Williams's baby out of the delivery room.

Josh administered Pitocin to Karen and started looking for lacerations. The episiotomy had extended well up into the rectum, and the right vaginal wall was a mess as a result of forceps injury and heavy bleeding.

Karen had lost a lot of blood, but she was going to live. What was she going to think, he wondered, when she saw the baby he had just delivered? It took him an hour to repair the devastation using four packs of suture.

The child was so strange, Josh thought. The eyes and hair seemed to blot out all other features in a way that he had never seen before.

Josh left the delivery room and checked in with Julie, telling her what had happened. Julie was dumbstruck, she nodded and tried to smile, but gave it up. She plopped down on her chair and stared straight ahead.

"Where's Jim?" he asked her. She nodded down the hallway, and finally, as he was starting to leave, she managed to say, "I'm sorry, Josh. It was terrible, wasn't it?"

"It wasn't good."

He entered the nursery and saw Jim Ellison's blond head hunkering over the table where Karen Williams's baby lay.

"Whaddaya think?" Josh said. Jim, startled, backed

away from the table. Josh looked past him and saw the child, I.V.'s draping its body, its life-support apparatus clamped in. Its skin was covered with red sores. The baby was not breathing. Josh shot a look at the monitor, which registered zero respiration, zero heartbeat.

"What the hell happened!" He rushed past Jim to the child and saw immediately that it was dead. He looked up at Jim, who looked dazed.

"I was walking by, looked in, found her. What *is* that?"

"Karen Williams's poor kid. Where's Birdsall?" He picked up the phone and barked an order to the desk. Birdsall came rushing in a moment later.

"What happened here?" Josh said.

Birdsall looked from one to the other accusingly. "This baby was healthy a minute ago. I got a stat on ward two—false alarm."

The three doctors stood around the table quietly staring down at Karen Williams's dead baby.

15

PAT MET FINANCIAL EDITOR KIT SINGLETON AT POUlos's, a Greek restaurant a half dozen blocks from the *Herald* offices. Pat told Kit she was nervous about running into Bill Walters or, worse, Harold Carey, and felt that she was persona non grata at the paper.

"That's ridiculous," Kit assured her as they sat together on the patio waiting for menus. "Everyone misses you and cannot understand why you made such a fuss."

"It was more than a fuss," Pat said. "I practically threatened to sue Walters and take the story to another paper." She flushed when she remembered the scene. It wasn't like her at all to scream threats at her boss—soon to be ex-boss, she supposed.

"You and every other senior reporter on staff." As Kit leaned across the table, her long black hair fell over her shoulders and her black upturned eyes were catlike in the glare from the street. "It's just that if a man yells at the boss they say he's tough, but if a woman does it, she's hysterical."

"Am I making too much of this, Kit?"

Kit shrugged. "I've certainly had my share of yelling sprees in Bill's office. I think I even broke something once."

Pat squeezed Kit's hand. She had always been a good friend. They traded ideas, did each other favors, went to bat for each other. There was a strong bond between them—if one was in trouble, the other would be there. They were like sisters fighting against the male-dominated rough-guy newsroom. Some of the men were jealous because both women had moved up faster than those guys who lolled around until they found themselves falling behind.

As financial editor, Kit's interests were out of Pat's realm, and Kit by her own admission couldn't tell a prognosis from a mitosis. On Pat's first day at the paper, Kit had steered her away from the "boob desk," the one closest to Harold's office. "You'll be the first person he sees when he storms out, hungry for blood. If you sit there, he'll suck you dry before he even learns your name."

The waiter brought over the menus, and Pat ordered a Greek salad with extra feta and a bottle of retsina. Kit ordered the same salad and passed on the wine.

"All right, you got me here," said Kit. "What's up?"

"I'm here to pick your brain."

"Manheim?"

"The very one."

"The thing is," Kit said, "I can't figure out why

you're so worked up about that series. I mean, why not drop it? I know it's your first, but we both know that Harold will give you another one right away. He owes you, and one thing about Harold, he pays up."

"There's a story here, Kit, and I suspect it's a big one."

"Why? Because Manheim was so hot to kill it? That's normal political bullshit. Very sensitive types, these candidates."

"I'm going ahead anyway."

"Okay." Kit took out her own notepad. "What do you want me to find out?"

"Financial background on Manheim—investments, stock holdings, hidden funds. Get me everything you can find."

"Anything in particular you're looking for?"

"I want to find out what happened to his money. He made millions from the orange grove sale, and I would like to know what he did with it."

"Got it." Kit smiled. "One Manheim special, with the works."

The wine arrived, and Pat slugged down the first glass and started on a second. Kit leaned back in her chair and smiled across the table at her. "Now I'd like to talk about another very important subject."

"What's that?"

"You."

Pat looked up at her, wondering if Kit could tell that she was pregnant. "Me?"

"We've been friends a long time . . ."

"No preamble. Out with it."

"Your hands are shaking. You're biting your fingernails. You're on your second glass of wine in under a minute. I know it's none of my business, but . . ."

Tears streamed from Pat's eyes. She grabbed her napkin and pressed it to her face. She saw people at other tables looking at her, but she didn't care. She felt Kit's hand. "Thank God for you," she said to her. "Sometimes I feel so alone."

"Okay, baby, how's that feel?" Josh looked up at Amy sitting in the saddle and handed her the reins. "Take it easy out there and try to stay in sight, okay?"

"Right, Daddy," she said, obviously not paying attention to anything he said and taking off like a shot toward the trees in back of the property. She was a very good rider, who preferred western style over English and loved to bushwhack. A real cowgirl. Greater love hath no man, Josh thought, watching her gallop off, the wind in her hair, her knees pressed against the sides of the pony. His little girl.

He started back inside when he saw dust kicking off the tires of a car coming down the road. As it drew closer he saw that it was a Jaguar. He knew only one person with a green Jag, and it was the one person he did not want around his house.

The car pulled into the drive, and Samantha Adams got out, wearing a business suit, her long hair flowing behind her. Rita Hayworth with a briefcase.

"Hello, Josh," she said, her head slightly bowed. She looked furtive; something was on her mind.

"I thought you were going away for the week," he said.

"I just needed a couple of days." She snapped her

fingers. "In and out, simple as that. May I come in?" When he hesitated, she added, "Just for a minute. You needn't worry. I'm not going to attack you." She held up a sheaf of papers. "I've got revisions on the program I gave you the other day. Honestly, it will only take a few minutes. Is your wife here?"

"No."

"All right, then." She brushed past him and through the screen door into the kitchen. He tagged along after her, wishing he could be more assertive sometimes.

He purposely stood on the opposite side of the butcher block from her, putting distance between them. She looked at him and said, "First, I have to apologize for the other day. I don't know what came over me. I overstepped my bounds." She leaned forward against the block. "From the first time I walked into your office I was inordinately attracted to you. Some things you can't control."

"Well, I'm flattered," he said, "but—"

"May I have something to drink?"

"Sure." He thought about wine, but that would have made this visit too social. "Soda?"

As he reached into the fridge for the bottle he felt her behind him, her fingers on his back.

"Josh." Her body was now pressed against him, her breath against his ear. "Just an affair. No strings attached. I travel all the time. I'm lonely. Just come and see me sometimes."

"Samantha, please, this is not—"

She took him by the shoulders and, with surprising strength, spun him around. She started kissing him. Her hands were all over him. And he could feel himself responding. Suddenly he realized that this was his kitchen. His daughter was outside. His wife was due back any minute.

He put his hands on Samantha's shoulders and pushed her away. "No!" he said and closed the refrigerator door behind him. "I'm going to have to ask you to leave."

She supported herself on the butcher block. He watched a tear run down her cheek. A silent moment passed between them. The sun cast a long shadow across the yard outside. Josh heard the hum of the refrigerator and the ticking of the wall clock his mother had given to him before she died.

Finally she said, "The papers are there," motioning to where she had left them on the table.

Josh waited. She straightened up and took her handbag from the table, then walked to the door. Turning back, she said, "I won't bother you any more. Good-bye, Josh."

He watched her stride across the lawn past Amy's toys and over the gravel to her car. The sun caught her hair and turned her pale green summer dress opaque in its light.

Samantha started the engine, and the long, sleek Jag moved like liquid around the drive and down the road. He stayed put for a few moments. Then he heard the engine again.

Through the screen door he saw that it was not the Jaguar but Pat's station wagon coming up the drive. He breathed a sigh of relief and went out to meet her.

"Who was that?" she said, handing him grocery bags.

"Who?"

"The redhead in the Jaguar. Who do you think?"

"The computer woman I was telling you about. She had some work to drop off before leaving town." At least that part of it was true, he thought.

Pat looked at her husband, wondering why he was so nervous. They walked past the screen door into the kitchen. She began taking the groceries out of the bags and putting them in the cupboards. "Why are you so jittery?"

He continued to help her to put the stuff away and then sat at the table looking out through the window.

"Something at the hospital?" she said.

"Isn't there always? No, I'm just generally nuts these days. How about you?"

I'm pregnant and don't know if I want the baby. Our marriage is on the rocks. And I'm on the verge of a nervous breakdown, can't you tell?

"This afternoon I met with Kit Singleton, the financial editor at the paper, and she promised to get me as much information on Manheim as she can. I'm going to have to meet with him again. He's getting ready to speak on the Senate floor in a few days, and I want to be there."

"In Washington?"

"Maybe even tomorrow, depending on when Kit can get me the info."

"Is this necessary?"

She put the last of the groceries away, poured herself a cup of coffee, and sat down next to Josh. "I want to prove to Bill Walters that I'm on top of this. Make him eat his words."

127

The phone rang, and Josh got up to answer it. "Yes, Barbara. How are you?" Then Pat watched his expression abruptly change to shock. "My God, you aren't serious." He cupped his hand over the receiver and mouthed, "Ted Tozian is dead." Back on the line, he listened, then slumped into the chair next to the phone. "Oh, Barbara, I'm so sorry. Of course, I'll be right out there. Catch a flight tomorrow. . . . I understand. . . . No, no problem. As soon as I make arrangements I'll let you know. . . . Good, good. Bye, Barbara."

Josh replaced the receiver and slouched back to the table. "Ted was trampled to death by his own horses. Barbara is out of her mind." His face took on a very odd expression, as if he had just realized something shocking. "This is the fourth death of one of my med school classmates in the last five months—Bart, David Morris, Gene, now Ted. I have to call the airlines."

"In a few minutes," she said. "First you're coming with me."

She led him out of the kitchen and through the foyer and up the stairs to their bedroom, where she laid him down and took off his clothes. She began kissing him—his lips, his hair, and along the gentle slope of his stomach. She could feel his resistance at first, and then he started to respond.

His eyes closed, and she saw the trace of a smile on his lips. She could almost feel the pressure drain out of him. "C'mon, baby, you know how good this is going to feel," she said.

A breeze blew in through the window. She took off her dress and underwear and stood over him, running her hands over her body, feeling the heat rise up in her. She reached between his legs and took his hard penis in her hand and stroked it. He let out tiny groans and started moving with her beat. "Right there," he said, "just like that."

She ran her fingers over his stomach and down along his thighs. He reached for her, and she felt his hands on her skin and the quiet sureness of his touch. When he was rock hard and she was wet, she climbed on top and straddled him, sitting down on him and rocking. "Now, isn't this just what we needed? Oh, yes," she said.

She rubbed her clitoris against him until she found the right spot and then she dug into him. Little moans escaped as she looked down at him. He was so handsome with his eyes half closed. "Come to Mama," she said. "Mama's gonna ride you good." He was so hard and deep in her she could barely stand the pleasure she was feeling. "You keep doing that, baby, this is gonna be a triple bagger." The shudders were coming faster as she felt him throbbing inside her. "I'm coming!" she shouted.

"I'm right behind you," he called out, and she slowed down to wait for him. Then she gasped and cried out. The spasms suddenly broke over her, and she let herself go. "Now!" Josh shouted. "Oh, God, now!"

"That's it, baby."

She was just a few seconds behind, thrusting harder

and harder. "Oh, Jesus!" she cried. And it came in rolling waves until she thought her head would blow off, and then she collapsed.

Pat lay quietly on top of Josh, listening to their breathing. This was the way it should be, she thought, and closed her eyes.

16

KELLY COX SAT NERVOUSLY IN THE WAITING ROOM FLIP-ping through a copy of *Parents* magazine. Every article warned against one thing or another. Drink milk, but don't drink too much. Take vitamins, but only those prescribed by your doctor. No pain reliev-ers, certainly no alcohol or cigarettes. Beware of too much sugar, too much protein, too much fat. I should just lock myself away, Kelly thought, and wait quietly for the next seven months.

Of course, there was an even longer and more confusing list of things to be done. Kelly had imagined that she only needed to buy baby clothes and a crib, maybe figure out which diaper service to use, and that would be that. Who would ever think, as one article suggested, that you had to start talking to your baby before the second month? Her husband Timmy had read the article and come home one night with a plastic funnel attached to a cord. He placed the funnel over her stomach and cooed into the cord. That way, he explained, the baby would get accustomed to his voice and years later, when the baby was going through some Oedipal crises, it would remember the comforting sound of its father's voice and everything would go so much more smoothly. Imagine!

It would be funny, ridiculous even, if it weren't for the shape inside her belly. She and Timmy had tried to have children for a year and a half before Dr. Ellison told her she might, at last, be pregnant. A parent could not laugh at something that might help or hurt a baby, however farfetched it seemed. So she found herself listening to calming music and practicing deep, controlled breathing. The French had done many studies proving how beneficial water was to infants, so she enrolled in a swimming class, even though she hated pools. Ocean swimming was, of course, too risky.

Kelly came to the end of the magazine and picked up another, automatically thumbing through the pages, eyes alert for the next warning article. The door opened and a woman entered with a young baby, maybe four months old.

"Hi," the woman said to her. "Are you waiting for Dr. Ellison?"

"Yes," Kelly said. "Dr. Heller is my usual doctor, but he's at the hospital, so Dr. Ellison is doing my checkup."

The woman smiled and held up her young son. "Don't worry," she said. "He delivered my Justin as easy as you please."

The baby gave a gurgle, and his mother burped him

gently against her shoulder. Kelly relaxed and smiled back. She knew that every delivery was different, but it reassured her to see how happy and healthy this mother and her son looked.

"That's so good to know," Kelly told the young woman. "I've been so anxious lately. Everything I do seems to be wrong."

"Your first?"

Kelly nodded. "I'm only two months along, but I feel as if I've been pregnant for years."

"That's always the way. This is my third, and I'll tell you something: the less you worry, the easier it goes."

Kelly held up a magazine article entitled "Negative Thoughts: Can Your Baby Hear Them?" "What about this?" she asked.

The woman laughed and handed her another magazine. "I'll tell you what to do with that—get it as far away from you as possible. Read this instead."

Kelly took the magazine and settled in happily with a copy of *Popular Mechanics.*

Twenty minutes later Julie came into the office calling Kelly's name. "Dr. Ellison will be with you in a minute. Follow me."

Julie led Kelly into an examination room and left her alone to undress and wait for the doctor. She sat on the edge of the table, the thin paper gown fluttering around her. The room was painted a pale pink, and there were baby pictures pinned to a corkboard along one wall. More successful deliveries, Kelly thought. The metal table that stood against the other wall made her nervous. So many hard little instruments, needles, and bottles. An I.V. rack was tucked into one corner, and a box of rubber gloves sat next to a smaller box filled with glass slides. Standard gynecological equipment, but to Kelly it was a cold reminder of the problems that could arise.

How was it, she thought, that this collection of metal and glass had anything to do with the pictures on the bulletin board? What did those indifferent instruments have to do with healthy babies? They looked more like torture devices or murder weapons.

"Hey, what's this?" The door opened and Jim Ellison walked in. "Is *Friday the Thirteenth* playing, or do you always look scared out of your wits?"

Kelly laughed in embarrassment. "I'm sorry, Dr. Ellison," she said. "One look at these instruments and everything and, well . . ."

"It's okay, Kelly." He walked over and picked up a tong-shaped tool. "Do you know what this is?"

"It's used for Pap smears, right?"

"That and other things. It's called a speculum. It looks scary, but it's constructed to open the passage in such a way that the least amount of pressure is applied."

Kelly relaxed a little and nodded.

"All of the things you see here," he said, "were designed to make you more comfortable. It's true, you could get through adolescence, become pregnant, and have your baby all without ever seeing a doctor. We don't do anything you can't do yourself; we just make it easier for you."

Kelly lay back and thought about Timmy and the baby they would have together. She felt Dr. Ellison doing whatever he was doing; he kept picking up little glass tubes and straight, hard, gleaming metal instruments. She felt a series of pinches and winced in pain.

"You okay?" he asked.

"Is everything all right?"

"Oh, yes, just seeing how baby is doing, and baby is doing fine."

Kelly went back to dreaming about her family's future, knowing that she was in good hands with the gentle-voiced Dr. Ellison.

17

PAT DIDN'T KNOW WHY SHE FELT THE NEED FOR SECRECY, but she did, and Kit, who laughed but didn't ask questions, had agreed to meet her at dusk under the Hillsborough Bridge. The river flowed down through Australian pines around the bend to where homeless men slept off last night's drunk, and down past construction sites and garbage dumps. The spot was so remote that police cruisers made only occasional passes, and chemical companies slipped in with dump trucks and unloaded their waste late at night. It was a beautiful spot, if you kept your eyes off the ground and trained on the treetops and the Tampa skyline.

With the temperature and humidity locked at 97, Kit had insisted they meet in her air-conditioned car.

"Paranoid?" Kit said to Pat when she climbed into the car.

"With Manheim and Walters after you, wouldn't *you* be?"

"I don't know about Walters, but with what I've found on Manheim, I would definitely stay away from that guy."

Pat pulled out her tape recorder and snapped it on. "You don't mind, do you?" she asked.

"Oh, in fact I do," Kit replied.

Pat looked at her colleague, surprised. "Are you serious?"

"Very."

Pat cocked her head toward Kit and raised an eyebrow.

"What I have here," said Kit, her voice low, "looks, at best, very shady. So if someone gets their hands on a tape recorder with my voice on it and wants to find the source . . ."

"Now who's paranoid?" Pat turned off the tape recorder and took a notebook and pen out of her handbag.

Kit turned to face her. "I have to tell you that I have not stopped digging since we talked. Manheim has left a very rocky trail, with roadblocks, detours, false leads, and dead ends. Thanks to the assistance of someone who shall go nameless, the path is now clear, and what a messy road it is. You're on to something, but I have to warn you, as my source warned me, you had better think long and hard before going ahead with this."

Pat said, "Thanks, but I'm committed."

"Which is what I thought you'd say. Okay, dear, hang on. You're about to hear a story." Kit took a cigarette and a gold lighter out of her red leather handbag, lit up, and inhaled deeply, her hollow cheeks and black eyes made her look more skeletal than usual.

"The way my source put it, tracing Manheim's millions makes the needle in the haystack look like a hot air balloon in a stadium." Kit glanced at the typewritten pages on her lap.

"Ten years ago, after Manheim's mother died and left him everything, he liquidated his assets within five months except for the small apartment he keeps here in Tampa and another in Washington. My source checked his taxes he paid on his Senate salary and a couple of investments. The man is Spartan and has been for a decade. He pays his bills, has his expense accounts. He's a regular upper-middle-class Boy Scout, so clean he's hard to read—too clean for my source, who went looking.

"She searched for audits, for trips he made, for anything that seemed out of the ordinary . . . and bingo, after about seven hours of rummaging she put a few things together and found gas station receipts and several expensive purchases made in McLean, Virginia. Nothing unusual there, except that Manheim paid for many of the purchases on a card belonging to the Sebastian Fund, a Virginia-based holding company."

"What is it, exactly?"

"Beats me. With more checking, my source turned up an office with a secretary. When my source found out that Manheim's father's name was Sebastian, the search naturally got more interesting." Kit crushed her cigarette in the ashtray and turned a page.

"It turns out that almost all the money in this

Sebastian Fund has been earmarked for something called the Humanitas Foundation."

"I'm confused," said Pat.

"You're supposed to be. Manheim set it up that way. The Humanitas Foundation supplies funds to many small companies, which are all part of or related in some way to a firm out in the woods near McLean called DNA, Inc."

Pat looked out the window—the bridge stanchions looked like little DNA ladders. "That's it," she said, feeling the prick of anticipation. "The link."

"And guess what DNA, Inc., makes?"

"Let me guess—widgets."

"Just about. Medical supplies."

"Medical supplies?"

"I have a list. Believe me, we could get this stuff in any store. They have sales and distribution; they have a few detail people on the road. A tidy little shop, nice little setup. But way too clean-looking, just like Manheim."

"And this is where his millions went?"

"To buy the land and build a medical complex with rolling hills and gardens and who knows what else?"

Pat thought for a moment. She had to get more on this company. "I've got to see Manheim. No more delays."

"My source advised against it. She said anybody who goes to that much trouble to hide his activities may be really dangerous and should be handled by the proper authorities."

"The proper authorities would be squelched in a

second. If Manheim found out about an official investigation, he would wipe the place clean, and they'd find nothing but medical supplies. No way."

Kit took her hand. "You know I'd do just about anything to get a story, but on this one there's just too much sitting in shadows for my taste. Or maybe, as my source says, DNA, Inc., really does make medical supplies, period. Don't be surprised if that's all there is."

"Sure."

"I would strongly advise you to get some help on this."

"Thanks, Kit. You've been a pal."

"Right."

"And don't look at me as if this is the last time you're going to see me alive."

"Don't read my mind," Kit replied.

On the drive home, Pat felt vindicated. Manheim was not on the level, and she was not off on some mad chase. But now she had to be clever and cagey without tipping her hand or making any amateurish mistakes. She would have to arrange with Jean Plessey to take care of Amy while Josh was in New Mexico and she was in Washington.

Her one objective was to find out what was behind DNA, Inc.

Before going home she decided to stop by the Waverly Inn and celebrate with a drink.

18

SHEETS OF RAIN SWEPT OVER THE CAR AS IT APPROACHED Tampa Airport's departure lanes. Pat was in turmoil; she wanted desperately to tell Josh about her pregnancy, but she couldn't. During the night she had worried about Manheim so much that she had gotten only a couple hours of sleep. Something else was bothering her—one of those nagging sensations that she could not quite identify. She was cranky, just waiting for Josh to retaliate so they could have a fight and she could win.

Amy, in the backseat, talked on about school and the ailments she thought her pony had. Fresh from medical texts in the library, she had decided to be a veterinarian when she grew up. After reading up on common ailments in farm animals, she was convinced that her pony was afflicted by them all.

"I love you," he whispered to Pat as he pulled in front of the terminal. "I'm going to miss you."

"Me, too," Pat said, pulling away, looking up into his eyes. "Give Barbara Tozian a big hug for me, would you? I'll be home day after tomorrow."

Amy leaned over the seat and wrapped her arms around her mother's neck. "Bye, Mommy," she said.

"Bye, darling, you take good care of Daddy and do whatever Mrs. Plessey says."

"I will. And don't take any guff from that Manheim character."

"You can bet on it."

Josh and Amy watched Pat until she vanished into the crowd.

Josh hurried home from the airport. He was already running late. Up in his bedroom, he took a dark suit out of his closet and fit the hanger inside a garment bag. He found a pair of black dress shoes in a box at the rear of his closet and threw them in as well. He wished Pat were here to help him with the choice of tie and shirt and to talk with him about Ted Tozian.

He and Ted had been close during their last year in medical school. In fact, Josh wondered if he would have chosen obstetrics and gynecology if Ted had not been so enthusiastic about the field. "The only way a man can get close to the experience of having babies," Ted used to say, "is by delivering them."

Josh sat on the bed, overwhelmed by the loss of his friend. He'd simply never imagined that someday he'd be going to Ted's funeral. A freak accident. He had a wonderful wife and kids, an excellent practice, a life any man would envy.

Josh was just about ready to go when he heard a cry

from the yard. Amy. He raced down the stairs and out the back door toward the barn.

Amy was on the ground beside her pony, her head cradled in the lap of . . . Samantha Adams! He reached her and knelt beside her.

Amy blinked up at him. "I slipped," she said, and managed to smile.

"I think it was the pony who lost his footing," Samantha said, stroking her head. "It happened just as I drove up."

Josh checked Amy's pupils for dilation, her legs and arms for fractures. "No broken bones," he said, relieved, "but look at that bruise on your shoulder."

"Oh, good," Amy said proudly. "Wait till I tell Jenny I was thrown!"

"You're going to have to wait a while for that," Josh said, "because right now you're going to bed."

Amy stared at him, unbelieving. "I thought I was going to Karen's."

"Going to Karen's right now is not a good idea."

"Please, Dad!" Amy pushed herself off the ground, attempting to stand, but she fell right back against Samantha.

"You're still woozy, dear," Samantha said. "You have to rest."

Amy's eyes closed involuntarily. "I want to go to Karen's. You'll be in New Mexico."

"Right now you had better stay put."

Samantha looked puzzled. "I didn't know you were leaving," she said.

Josh explained about the funeral as he lifted Amy

143

into his arms and carried her toward the house. They settled her in her bedroom with a pile of pillows around her and a stack of Pat's fashion magazines. Samantha went down to the kitchen and reappeared with an enormous silver tray that Pat used for dinner parties. She balanced the tray across Amy's lap with the flourish of a headwaiter.

The contents of the tray were hidden beneath several linen napkins, which Samantha made a game of lifting off one by one.

"Let's see." Amy's hands ran over a napkin, trying to gauge the shape of the thing underneath. "It's got a smooth top, and bumpy legs! I know. The butter dish!" Amy lifted the napkin off and revealed the silver butter dish.

"But what's inside?" Samantha asked.

"Butter?" Amy laughed as she lifted the lid and revealed four double-stuffed Oreo cookies.

As Samantha and Amy continued the game, discovering strawberries in a bread basket and a can of Coke inside a sock, Josh was amazed at how easily Samantha had won Amy's confidence. Amy was usually shy with strangers, especially adults.

"Daddy, can she?" Amy asked.

"Can she what?" Josh said.

"You never listen; Mom's right." Amy shook a finger at him. "Samantha said she could stay with me until Mrs. Plessey comes home. Then you could go away like you planned. Please?"

"I wouldn't mind staying with her until Mrs. Plessey comes home, really."

"Why exactly did you come over here?" Josh said.

"In the confusion of the other day," she explained, "I forgot to give you the disks."

She picked up her briefcase from Amy's bedside table and took out a packet. "I didn't know you were going out of town, so I brought them." She handed them over. "But they don't seem very important, after Amy's fall."

"If these are half as good as the others, I'll have the most efficient office in Tampa. Thank you."

"What about it, Dad?" Amy asked from her bed. "Can Sam stay with me until Mrs. Plessey comes home?"

Samantha sat on the edge of Amy's bed. "Of course, I'm staying. That's all there is to it."

"I can't ask you, really . . ."

"To be honest, I brought these disks over because I wanted you to see them, but I wanted to see you, too."

"And me?" Amy asked.

"You," Samantha said, patting Amy's legs through the coverlet, "are a bonus." She looked squarely at Josh. "There are times when I'm lonely living by myself. You're very lucky to have such a lovely family."

"Yeah!" Amy cheered from the bed. "Daddy, go pack. What time's the plane?"

Josh checked his watch. "Three-forty. I can still make it."

"Are you packed?" Samantha asked.

"Five minutes."

"I'll come down and say good-bye."

Amy giggled from the bed. "I'll come down, too."

It was a huge relief to see Amy happy. Josh knew it

145

was easy to overprotect an only child. He struggled constantly to allow her to do the most ordinary things. He did not want to leave her, but she was having so much fun with Samantha that it would probably upset her more if he stayed home.

"Okay, honey," he said. "I'm going to leave you in Miss Adams's hands. But if I find out you've tried to take advantage in any way—"

"Daddy, I won't!"

"All right, then. Samantha, you're sure?"

"It will be my pleasure. We'll have fun, won't we, Amy?"

"You bet!"

"Accidents can buzz around the body in ways you don't know about," Josh told her. "I'm not going to leave unless you promise to sleep."

He had expected her to protest, but she lay back on her pillows, eyelids at half mast. He leaned over and kissed her. "Bye, honey, see you in two days." Samantha took Josh's arm and led him out of the bedroom.

In the hallway she let go of Josh's arm reluctantly. "Finish your packing," she told him, "and I'll meet you downstairs."

Josh had only a few minutes to marvel over the strange twist in events. He was going to his friend's funeral without his daughter, who was staying home not with his wife but with his computer rep. He zipped up the garment bag and lugged it downstairs.

"You look good enough to eat," Samantha said.

"How should I take that?" he replied. "Look, you're sure about Amy? You can still back out."

"I'll be happy to watch her. It's a partial repayment for the way I acted the other day. I'm here not to create problems but to solve them." She held out her hand. "Peace?"

"Peace is always a good idea," he said, taking her hand.

She looked up at the wall clock. "You had better get going."

Before climbing into the car he looked up at Amy's second-floor bedroom window. She had pressed her face against the glass, and was waving good-bye. He blew her a kiss, climbed in, and drove away.

19

THE SUN WAS JUST SETTING, AND HER DADDY'S PLANE WAS on its way to New Mexico when Amy was awakened by the phone. When she sat up, a pain shot across her left shoulder that made her head hurt. Down the hall she heard Samantha say hello.

Amy sneaked downstairs very carefully, picked up the living room extension, and heard her mother's voice. It was all she could do to keep from interrupting the conversation and telling her mother about this afternoon.

"Amy is resting now," Samantha said. "She had a little accident, and Josh asked me to stay with her until Mrs. Plessey comes home."

"Accident! What are you talking about?" Amy could hear the panic in her mother's voice.

"She fell off her pony—slipped off, really. Nothing was injured; she just seemed woozy. I happened to drop over with some work, so I offered to stay."

"Who are you?" Amy heard her mother say angrily.

Samantha did not sound very friendly; her voice was cold. "I'm a business associate of your husband's, Mrs. Heller. My name is Samantha Adams. I imagine Josh has mentioned me."

"Do you know what time his flight lands in Santa Fe?"

"I'm afraid not," Samantha said.

"Well then, please tell Amy I miss her and that I'll call her tomorrow."

"I will." Samantha practically barked that into the phone. Then, to Amy's amazement, she heard the receiver click. Samantha had hung up on her mother.

Amy thought Samantha sounded funny. Something was wrong, but Amy could not quite figure out what. She decided to go back upstairs and see what she could find out.

Upstairs, Amy crept along the carpet strip. She heard a noise from down the hall—drawers opening and closing. Her slippers crept like little mice along the carpet.

The door to her parents' bedroom was open a crack, and inside she saw Samantha searching through her father's file cabinet, removing papers and looking at them, then returning them to their proper place.

The phone rang again, but this time Samantha ignored it. It rang again and again. Amy thought it might be her mom again. She wanted to answer it, but she was afraid. The little girl studied Samantha carefully, trying to figure out why she was searching through the cabinet. She was determined to find out.

Amy backed down the hallway to her room where

she stood in the hallway outside her door. After taking a big breath, she made a sound like clearing her throat. "Samantha?" she called. "Samantha?"

A few seconds later Samantha poked her head out into the hall. "Yes, Amy?"

"I feel a lot better now," she said in her most grown-up voice, "and I want to thank you for taking care of me, so let's drive down to the Frosty Freeze. I'll buy you a milk shake." As an afterthought, she said, "And I won't take no for an answer."

Amy sensed danger here, as if Samantha were some kind of spy. She was determined not to let the woman out of her sight until she had the answer.

20

IT WAS THE WORST FLIGHT JOSH HAD EVER TAKEN. THE man on his right, a toy salesman, never stopped talking, except to slug down Bloody Marys. When the man fell asleep he snored so loud that the flight attendants had to wake him up. The woman to his left emitted an odor that made Josh feel nauseated. Tomatoes? Urine? Perfume of some awful kind, made out of prunes? Who knew? The woman smelled like the pabulum Amy used to throw around the kitchen. When the plane landed, Josh wanted a shower.

The Santa Fe air, as advertised, was soft and almost frivolous. The famous light that drew painters from all over the world with their easels and canvases and brushes made him forget the awful flight. Everything was so stark, clear, and precise that it looked like a videotape to him, as if God himself had drawn thin stark lines around every object before filling in the color.

With a map in one hand and the steering wheel of his rented car in the other, he headed due west toward the foothills of the Nacimento Mountains. The closer he got to the Catholic church where the funeral service would be held, the clearer his memories of Ted Tozian became.

Ted had spent as much time philosophizing about human anatomy as he did studying it for exams. Ted's eyes were always darkly rimmed, as if he had not slept in days. Ted was a brooder. He would sit in his upper-floor window drinking espresso, memorizing the parts of the human body and their functions.

Josh remembered the night he had gone up to ask Ted a question and had found Barbara, Ted's girlfriend then, stretched out naked on a specimen table, legs spread, in a harness, holding a medical text. Ted was down between her legs with a light poking around, reeling off the parts of her anatomy in preparation for a gynecology exam the next morning.

When Josh walked in, all they did was glance at him nonchalantly. Ted asked him to hang around a minute. Barbara went back to the text, spot-checking Ted's answers: "Right. Right. Nope. Try again. That's right. Next."

Memories of medical school flooded over Josh as he drove along the ribbon of highway that wove through mesa flats and pink desert under Technicolor skies. Whirls and wisps of clouds sailed toward an infinite horizon as heat waves pirouetted off the red earth.

St. Jude's, a small adobe church, stood beside a lake and was overhung by one of the most sorrowful cottonwood trees Josh had ever seen. The setting reminded him of an old John Ford movie. The parking lot was filled with late-model Land Rovers, Cherokees, and trucks—the latest in doctors' vehicles. Men and women dressed in black milled around outside the church door, while others strolled in couples by the lake.

St. Jude's was right out of Ralph Lauren's Old West. Serapes, cactus pots, bleached cattle horns, and designer pews. The rugged-looking, square-jawed priest had a dark gutted face and big hands that looked as if they had been breaking horses for years. He spoke with a west Texas twang.

Throughout the service, and later at Ted and Barbara's house, Josh's attention was drawn to a short, round man with thinning blond hair and pale skin who kept wringing his hands and fidgeting as if he were on amphetamines. Josh asked Rod Hardesty, the medical school class wit, who the man was.

"Ted's partner, Rex Wilkes," Rod said. "But I'll tell you this: Wilkes is not the same guy I met a few months ago. Back then he was nice and pleasant, hands didn't shake. I had a conversation with him about lap zaps."

Josh walked over to Wilkes and introduced himself.

"Oh, yes, of course," said Wilkes. "Ted talked about you. You're down in Georgia or somewhere."

"Florida. Rex, what was going on with Ted that he allowed himself to get caught in a barn with his own horses? He knew those animals well, didn't he? He'd been riding all his life."

"I don't know how well he got along with them. I'm not fond of horses," Rex replied.

153

"Was anything troubling Ted? Problems at the office?" Josh looked around to make sure Barbara Tozian wasn't nearby. "Trouble at home?"

"What's with the interrogation?" Wilkes snapped.

"I'm just asking questions—"

"Which the police have already asked."

"Ted was an old friend. If you don't want to talk to me, just say so," Josh said calmly.

"Why are you bothering *me* with this!" Rex screeched.

"Take it easy, Rex," Josh said.

"He was my friend, too, and I cared a great deal about him. You don't have any right to make accusations."

"What accusations?"

"You are obviously trying to discredit me, and I will not accept it. You do not have any evidence."

Josh reached out to touch Wilkes's arm, to cool the man down, but Wilkes jumped back, shaking like a caged animal.

"Wilkes—"

"I didn't want to keep doing it. I didn't."

Josh gaped at the nervous doctor, wondering where this new twist was leading. "Keep doing what?"

"There was nothing else I could do." Wilkes lowered his head and muttered. "I really must go. Goodbye." With that he spun on his rubber-soled shoes and marched away.

Wally Lopez was a pretty, shy woman of about thirty-five who had been Ted Tozian's nurse for six years. Josh was struck by her large brown eyes floating in tears. Her black hair, streaked with gray, had fallen out of its barrette and hung over her face. She seemed to be spending most of her time drying her eyes with a big pink bandanna.

Josh found her huddled in a corner of Barbara Tozian's kitchen speaking Spanish with a woman who looked like her sister. When Josh approached, the woman touched Wally lightly on the arm and excused herself.

"Wally?" Josh said to her, "I'm Josh Heller. Ted and I went to medical school together."

"I am pleased to meet you," Wally said through her tears.

"I know this is a bad time to ask questions. I hope you don't mind."

Wally sneezed and Josh plucked a Kleenex out of a box on the counter and handed it to her. He said, "I just had a talk with Dr. Wilkes . . ."

"He's in bad shape," Wally said, rolling her eyes. "He talks all the time about I don't know what. In the past few days he's been loco, running around blaming himself for things. I don't know why he feels responsible or guilty for what happened to Dr. Ted."

"What was happening with Ted that made him so careless?"

Wally peered up at him from under her thick brows. "Lot of problems," she said. "Mothers and babies dying, coming out wrong."

"Coming out wrong?"

"Wrong color, wrong sex, wrong babies, wrong everything. Everything was a mess. Dr. Ted was very unhappy. The word was getting out, and his patients were canceling."

"You say 'wrong babies.' Can you give me examples?"

"First the computer broke down, and I was getting information that wasn't even mine. Women were fine in the afternoon and dying at night. Babies were delivered with rashes or tumors where none were indicated earlier. Babies with red hair and green eyes—a lot of those. It was like the Twilight Zone, Dr. Heller. You can't imagine."

"Oh, I can indeed."

The woman who had left her side was back, scowling at Josh.

What was this, he thought, a replay of his own situation? Business collapsing, patients canceling, pregnant women losing their babies or giving birth to infants they swore were not their own.

Through the crowd of people Josh spotted blond, open-faced Barbara Tozian standing by the china cabinet, looking helpless.

"Hello there," he said, trying for some cheer.

"Hello, Josh, pull up a tear."

"How are you holding up?"

"It's been one shock after another." When she faced him he saw anger in her eyes. "Isn't this great?" she said. "I don't know how I'm supposed to feel, what I'm expected to feel. The only man I've ever loved is dead, and part of me is glad."

"Glad?"

"Well, thank God I'm not the last to know. You're the only fool in town, Josh."

"Why don't you sit down?" he said, leading her to a couch. When they were seated and Barbara had sipped some wine, Josh said, "Talk to the only fool. I'm listening."

Barbara raised her chin, stared out into the desert light, and said softly, "My darling husband died in the midst of a torrid affair."

"Oh, Jesus."

"Some hot dame he met through business or something. I haven't got all the details, and I don't want to know them, to tell you the truth. I took the kids to my mother's—what a cliché, huh?—while he got laid a lot. I hate him, miss him, don't want him gone. I'd take him back in a second." She gave a funny little laugh. "Isn't that a ridiculous thing to say? Oh, God." She drained her glass and put it down on the coffee table.

"Couldn't help himself—that's how he put it. The man could control his bladder better than anyone and had more discipline than a Buddhist monk, but he couldn't help himself when it came to a chick in fuck-me pumps."

"Where is this home-wrecker now?" Josh asked. Samantha abruptly entered his thoughts, unsettling him.

"Probably out screwing somebody else. She doesn't care, obviously. Or maybe she's smart enough to know that I'd kill her. Nobody seems to know anything about her. Some sleazy town girl he met in a motel or something. A detail rep from a pharmaceutical company. Who knows?"

"How did you find out about her?"

"Ted blurted it out a few nights ago. Said he needed help. He was obsessed—'strung out like a junkie' is how he put it. How do you think I felt? Was I supposed to pat him on the head and say, 'There, there, Teddy, put your thing back in your pants and don't see her again'? No, like a jerk, I screamed at him, gathered up the kids, and left. I told him when he was done with Dolly to make sure to call. Then maybe he could have his family back."

"He must have been a mess."

Barbara turned and said, "I know he was. Thinking back on it, I realize he was crying out for help, and I said go screw yourself and left. I didn't realize. If I had, Josh, he would be alive, wouldn't he?"

Josh took her hand. "I don't know. The thing that bothers me is the accident. Ted knew horses, for crying out loud. He would not have allowed them to trample him."

"Freak accidents happen."

"Freak accidents." Josh did not like the sound of that. "What about his partner, Dr. Wilkes? What's his story?"

"The guy's like a robot. Lives alone, no girlfriend, no friends in general. But he's one heck of a doctor. I mean, always there, always cheerful, no complaining. Well educated."

"Sounds like my own partner," said Josh. "Except that I just talked with Wilkes, and he seems to have gone a little nuts."

"If you lost a partner, wouldn't you? What's a husband? You can always replace them, but a good partner . . . Am I being cynical?" She smiled. Her anger subsided. "I *am* being cynical. I am also beat, so can I go and lie down? Make yourself comfortable, and thanks for coming, Josh."

After he gave her a hug and she went upstairs, Josh carried his wine outside and stood on the back veranda staring at the desert pastels and the red buttes. He thought about Samantha's proposition. How easy it would have been to accept. How disastrous. He could understand Ted's obsession. When he thought about Samantha he felt an ache in his loins, but nothing beyond that. He knew he could not have the apple without accepting the responsibility for eating it. He also knew that he could have crossed that line very easily in the pool. It was so easy to lose control.

What had Rex Wilkes said about not being able to control himself? From doing what?

Josh went back inside and dialed home, but there was no answer. He called Jean Plessey next door. She said she had not seen Amy and the house was dark. At the hospital, Julie said she had not seen Samantha Adams. When a call to Sam's home went unanswered, Josh began to worry. He called the airline and was told he might get an earlier flight on standby.

"Mad?" he heard the voice behind him say.

He turned and found himself looking at Dr. Rex Wilkes. "I can't find my daughter or my wife—or anybody, for that matter."

"I am sure they're all right."

"How would you know?" he snapped. Then, realizing how he must have sounded, Josh apologized. "Sorry. Been under a lot of pressure."

"We all have," Wilkes said dully.

"Especially Ted. Did you know he had a mistress?" Josh caught the flicker of a lie when Wilkes said no.

"You don't know if he had one or you don't know if you want to tell me about it?"

"You're trying to be clever."

"One of my oldest friends just died under mysterious circumstances—"

"Nothing mysterious about horses bolting," Wilkes said.

"To me there is. Now, one more time, Doctor: did he have a girlfriend?" Josh waited for Wilkes to respond. Instead, the man stood there as if petrified.

Wilkes seemed to go into a trance. Then, after suddenly snapping out of it, he said, "I wasn't able to do anything about it, Dr. Heller. Please believe me when I say that. I cared very much for Ted, but there are things, powers, that I could not control."

"What powers? You weren't able to say no to what, Rex?"

"You'll know soon enough, Dr. Heller. Believe me. And now if you'll excuse me, I have to go. Good-bye."

Josh followed him out. "Wilkes, wait a minute."

But Wilkes was scurrying across the living room and through the front door. By the time Josh got outside, Wilkes was driving away in a blue Chevrolet.

Josh stood on the front porch leaning against a wooden post, sweat pouring down his face.

CHRISTMAS BABIES

He listened to the din of conversation inside, watched a herd of shadows slide across the desert as clouds passed beneath the sun. He sat down on the steps, bringing his knees to his chest, and rocking.

Then he closed his eyes and felt the Santa Fe heat take hold.

21

WHENEVER PAT GOT NERVOUS AND HAD A LOT OF THINK-ing to do, she shopped.

A new dress, shoes, hat, bag, and accessories, a gold bracelet with matching earrings, cosmetics. But whenever Pat spent over a hundred dollars on anything she felt guilty. Frugality was next to godliness in her upbringing. She felt, though, that she often went beyond frugality into being just plain cheap. The dollar, for her parents, who had saved all they made and resisted every extravagance, became the family icon. They prayed for, fought over, drank over, and finally died for the buck. Pat had watched its effect, and at some point, in her adolescent mind, she had decided that the gravity of a dollar bill would not weigh as heavily on her as it did on them.

This afternoon she had forced her way through prudence into believing that she truly wanted, and deserved, something new. She hadn't bought clothes in years, at least nothing as sophisticated as this. After all, where did she and Josh go except to medical conventions and out to dinner, if they could find a sitter.

Still the guilt was there, but to her surprise it was magically dispelled when she left the store, wearing her new outfit and stepped into the Georgetown sunlight where she felt as if she belonged among the elegant women parading by.

She dressed well. After all, she was scheduled next morning to meet Mr. Wonderful. She was nervous about the meeting at the Senate Office Building. Even though she hated to admit it, she felt a certain awe at being here in the nation's capital to meet face to face with one of its titans. She reminded herself not to be too awestruck. Manheim was involved in shady dealings. Her job was to shine a bright light on the senator's dirty work.

"It's strictly business," Josh had reminded her. "Play it that way and save yourself a lot of aggravation."

Pat decided to stop for a cappuccino down the street at a sidewalk café. She chose a table under a cluster of green and white umbrellas behind vertical latticework and ferns. From her seat she could watch the procession of people pass by. Instead of a cappuccino she ordered a vodka gimlet, remembering vaguely the promise she had made to herself not to drink.

The more she drank, the more Pat felt justified in nailing this phony crusader. But after the second gimlet all she wanted to do was go back to her hotel room and be alone for a couple of days. With the third gimlet her confidence returned and she felt that she could win any battle. She would beat Manheim and Walters, and have the baby by herself if necessary.

She didn't need Josh and his evasiveness. Why was he evasive? she wondered, and then her thoughts turned to other questions. Why had he been so touchy lately? Why had he been secretive about his comings and goings? Who was the woman she had seen him with at the Hilton? And who was the young redhead with the straight back and the alabaster skin driving the Jaguar out of their driveway? Who was the one who had answered the phone when she called home. In a flash of insight, she knew exactly what his secret was. It was so damned obvious! Josh had another woman! No wonder he had hemmed and hawed. No wonder he had changed the subject so quickly.

Samantha Adams. The computer genius. And now Amy's baby-sitter. Taking care of the little darling, *at Josh's insistence!* So that she and Josh could do what? Obviously to say good-bye to good old expendable Pat Heller, former newspaper medical writer and current drunk. The courts would give Josh custody of Amy, and when Samantha took her place beside Josh, who would Amy want to be with? Who else?

She ordered another drink. This *had* to be her imagination, she thought, but why did everything seem so logical? That's what had been bothering Josh—how to let her down gently, how to let her know about this beautiful young doll with her own company and money in the bank. She remembered seeing them at the Hilton, where they had been sitting together like lovers. And now the bitch had her daughter and was probably showering her with gifts, turning her against her own mother.

My God, she thought, I'm losing everything. My job. My husband. My daughter. My life. She couldn't stand her thoughts anymore and called for the check. She did not know what she was going to do, but she knew she had to get out of Washington.

She stumbled out of the café and down the street. People stared at her. Pat Heller, drunk. She felt lost without her family. Here in this alien city all she had was a sterile hotel room filled with corporate furniture, a corporate painting of a leaf over the bed, soap wrapped in paper, a plastic shoe horn, and a tub that was too small.

She was certain, as she walked through the fading sunlight down M Street, that the people passing by noticed the tears in her eyes and the blotches on her skin.

The only thing Pat knew for sure was that she needed sleep. Now the only problem was the hotel—she couldn't remember its name.

She stood in the middle of M Street and searched through her bag. She found nothing with the hotel name on it, no matches, no receipt. But she did find an austere looking card with Curt Manheim's telephone number.

Well, she thought, she did know somebody in this city after all, the good senator himself. She wondered what he was doing at this moment, and thought that maybe the *Herald*'s star medical reporter should find out.

22

THE SKY MATCHED HIS MOOD. THE PAINT JOB ON THE GA-rage was the same color as his disposition. The hair at his temples was the shade of his future. All gray, all dull, all irritating. Josh Heller hated gray because gray was nothing, it was neither here nor there, and he did not give a damn that gray was the universal color of oneness for the Zen mind. He did not feel oneness with anything right now, he felt separateness. Things were definitely falling apart—raining in little gray fragments from the formerly secure roof of his exis-tence.

Josh called from the Tampa airport and nobody was home. He got into the car and drove through the heat back to his house on the edge of town. The sun was a blood orange over the Gulf of Mexico, dripping into the thin line of horizon. Sea gull squadrons soared above him. It was after five, and the sprinkler systems could now legally be turned on to water the brown, drought-dry lawns.

He drove through his neighborhood of bright two-story homes with wooden facades and tired bushes, big yards and new cars.

He passed his house and headed down the way to Jean Plessey's. A jet black Nissan four-by-four, a dump truck with Plessey Construction on it, two dirt bikes for the kids, and Dad's BMW road bike were parked in the driveway. The Plesseys owned every modern American techno-toy.

The Plesseys were sitting around the table heartily eating their meat and mashed potato American dinner: Jean, her husband, and two overweight kids. He asked them about Amy.

"I guess she hasn't come back yet," Jean said. Her cheeks were big and red, and her clothes fit too snugly. Jean had a square, kindly face, and you knew you could rely on her.

"Back?" Josh said. "From where?"

Her husband, with a bottle of Pabst before him, looked up and waved. "What's the trouble, Doc?" He was a big man with a $200,000-a-year income from building industrial parks.

"Do you know where she went?" Josh asked.

"No idea. The woman said she would take care of everything," Jean said.

Samantha, Josh thought. "Did the woman mention where she was taking Amy?"

"Not a word, but to tell you the truth, the woman said very little, didn't seem to want to chat at all. I did speak with the neighbors and told their kids to keep an eye on the house, just in case. Where's Pat?"

"Still in Washington, D.C. You go back to supper, and thank you."

Jean Plessey walked outside with Josh. She placed a hand on his arm. "Is everything all right, Josh? You look frazzled."

"It's been frantic the past few days."

"Have you tried . . . the police? I could have Rodney call the chief for you at home, get a quick answer."

"I'm sure everything is okay. I'll let you know, Jean, thanks."

Back at home Josh went up to Amy's room. Her bed was made. Everything was in its place, and the room was even a little neater than it usually was.

He went out the back door and through the covey of green and white lawn furniture to the barn. The pony was in her stall, but it had no food and no water. Josh fed it and let it out into the exercise ring behind the barn.

He returned to the house and called Samantha, but there was no answer. It was getting dark outside, and the streetlights had snapped on. He removed his jacket and tie, draped them over the back of a kitchen chair, and poured himself a glass of milk.

He got Pat's hotel number off the bulletin board by the phone and called. The clerk put him through to her room; no answer. He left a message. He picked up the phone and dialed again.

"Hello?"

"Julie?"

"Josh, where the heck are you?"

"Right here, at home. Julie—"

"We have been looking for you everywhere. All hell has broken loose at the hospital. Abby Golding. Lynn Rozelle. Carrie Billings. A prenatal horror show. Jim's down there now, doing what he can. I've been up all night, had to come home to change clothes, and I'm going right back down again."

Josh leaned back against the kitchen wall, took out his handkerchief, and rubbed it across his mouth. "Have you heard from Amy?"

"No. Where's she supposed to be?"

"With Samantha Adams."

"The bimbo?"

"Amy fell off her pony and hurt herself, and Samantha—"

"I worry about that one."

"I can't find Amy, Julie."

"She'll show up. She's a big girl. So's Samantha."

"You don't sound convinced."

"I'm going back to the hospital. You look for Amy. We have backup. Jim called Mike Ward to assist. So keep your spirits up and get there when you can. You got that?"

"I got it."

"Good-bye. Call me every once in a while, would you?"

Josh knew he had to think clearly and not panic, which was not going to be easy. He made a list of possibilities, edited the list, cut it even more, until he found himself staring at the only remaining possibility.

He got out of the chair and walked outside and

across the lawn to his car, knowing exactly where he had to go.

In a sophisticated Virginia medical facility four children died under strict laboratory conditions, and that was the good news. The mouse viruses had malfunctioned again and made the genetic transfer a nightmare.

Sores the size of silver dollars had spread out like tiny sunbursts on the children's skin.

The chief lab physician had not wanted to deliver the news to the director, so he had taken it upon himself to use an experimental carrier molecule that tested well in animals. The initial results had been so positive that he went ahead and used the same carrier on three other infants.

At this point, all seven babies lost their respiratory abilities, their hearts stopped beating, and they died.

The chief lab physician informed the director, who ordered him to incinerate the children's bodies and get back to work.

After the physician left, the director picked up the telephone, dialed, and ordered the party on the other end of the line to procure more subjects for him.

23

PAT'S HEADACHE WAS MONUMENTAL. THE PAIN STARTED out as a small dark spot in the center of her brain, at the tail end of a dream that faded so fast she could barely remember it. As the dark spot grew, it was replaced by bright splashes of light until the light overtook the darkness. Great numbing gobs of pain plunged down upon her, hurt her eyes, and made her want to run.

Then came the tears, flowing uncontrollably. What in the living hell is the *matter* with me! she thought. *"Stop this!"* she said through the tears.

She had to go to the bathroom, but could not drag herself across the room. Room? she thought. What room? For a moment she didn't know where she was, and not really caring, she drew the covers over her head.

Her mouth was filled with balls of dry foam like the kind that protected things in the mail.

She let one foot slip out from under the covers to search around until she found the floor, then she dragged out the other. Her arms moved out from their hiding places into the air. A light blazed from across the room, and as she peeked at it she recognized the draperies and realized that she was in her own hotel room. Thank God.

Pat stumbled to the bathroom. Sitting on the john and staring dumbfoundedly through the doorway into the bedroom she saw something that made her forget about her pain for the moment. Her clothes. Neatly folded on the chair, Her shoes, side by side, at the foot of the bed. Her handbag, on the dresser, next to her hat. She was never this tidy.

She looked down and realized that she had nothing on. She never went to bed naked. Pat was frightened; she could remember nothing of last night except her feeble attempt to walk home from the café. She squeezed her eyes closed and tried to piece together a sequence of events that might help explain this uncharacteristic neatness. How did she get back? How did she get into bed? Why was she naked?

Through the open bathroom door she saw the message light blinking. After traipsing back into the bedroom, her hand shaking, she punched in the number and asked the operator who had called.

"Four calls from your husband," the woman said, "and two from Senator Curtis Manheim's office."

Pat looked at her watch and jewelry lying side by side on the end of the dresser. She was not this tidy, ever. "Thank you," she said and picked up the watch, which read 9:40. Her appointment with Manheim was for eleven. She would never make it.

Manheim? Manheim? Why did she have such a vivid impression of him? She called the hotel operator back and asked her when the Manheim calls had come in. One at seven-thirty, another at eight. This morning. How did the senator know where she was staying?

She closed her eyes and there, through the fog, was a memory of Manheim sitting across a table from her. The room was dark, with low light. A band played. The waiter was a tall man in formal wear, and there were couples dancing. She watched herself get up and walk unsteadily past the waiter to a bathroom where she . . . fell down?

She carried these strange thoughts with her back into the bathroom and stood under the shower, picking her way through her memory.

There was a car, and a backseat, and there was Manheim again, solicitous, charming, and very handsome in the half-light. He wore a dark suit, his nails were manicured, and his touch was gentle. She froze. He touched her; Pat could almost feel his fingers on her shoulders, her bare shoulders.

She unconsciously made the water hotter, scalding. Bare hands on bare shoulders. "Oh, God!" she shouted, seeing the senator right in front of her face, leaning into her, a questioning look stitched into his brows; he was asking her something.

She threw back the shower curtain expecting to see him, but there was nothing but bare bathroom tile.

After calling home and getting no answer Pat called

173

her husband's office. She asked Julie to please have Josh call the hotel when he got in. She hoped Amy was off at school and that her husband was still in New Mexico. She ordered breakfast from room service and waited until it arrived—twenty minutes later. She drank two glasses of orange juice and three cups of coffee to subdue her dehydration, and then she got up the courage to call Curt.

Thinking of him as Curt now? How familiar of you, she thought as she waited.

A woman answered the phone, "Senator Manheim's office." Pat identified herself and the operator put her through.

"Well, there," he said, "and how are you this morning?"

"Just fine, thank you. I'm, uh . . . calling to apologize, to tell you that I don't think I'll be able to get in before noon."

He laughed, a hearty politician's laugh, which to Pat's hung-over ears sounded almost authentic. "We're still having lunch at Jasper's, aren't we?"

A pause. Lunch at Jasper's? Pat remembered something about that phrase. His mouth moving: Lunch at Jasper's. One o'clock. Forming those very words.

"Hello?" he said.

"I'm afraid I'm a little under the weather this morning."

"I don't doubt it."

Another pause. How does he know so much, or sound as if he does? Pat wondered.

"Senator . . ."

"How soon we forget."

174

"I beg your pardon?"

Now it was his turn to be silent. Then: "You don't remember?"

"Remember what?"

"That we . . . last night . . ."

My God! The images suddenly flew at her, shards of memory racing by her eyes. She could feel his heat, the broad face rising up and filling the screen in front of her. The big lips, the gentle dog eyes, and the hair that was always in place. From the darkness of the back-seat of a car. And the room, the low-light room somewhere . . .

"I think I'd better hang up . . . No, not yet." She didn't want to do that. "I drank a lot last night . . . or got sick. I must have been sick. . . . There was a small café on M Street where I had something. . . . My God, this is terrible!"

"You were angry," he said, a softness in his voice.

"I was." A statement, not a question. "Maybe we should meet after all."

"I'll send the car for you."

"That won't be necessary." She could hear the defensiveness in her own voice.

"You know Roger. He'll be downstairs waiting for you at one."

I know Roger, she thought, his chauffeur? What *had* happened last night? A blackout. She wondered if she should ask him about the evening. "All right," she agreed, "one o'clock."

She sat on the bed and looked out through the window to a park across the street where children played and nurses pushed strollers. Streams of traffic raced by. She wanted to go back to sleep. If she had not been drunk last night she would have been studying the research she had brought to grill Senator Curt Manheim with. But instead there was a much more important matter to concern herself with—piecing together last night.

Pat looked at the clock; she had three hours to remember.

Roger was a mystery to her. She had no memory of ever having met or seen him. He was a tall, thin man of about forty-five with a Ronald Colman mustache and long slender fingers. His short brown hair was plastered against the sides of his head, and his dull blue eyes never blinked.

"Mrs. Heller," he said, "how nice to see you again." She searched for something sly or devious in his expression but found nothing.

"Thank you." She followed him out of the lobby and down the stairs to the waiting blue limousine. Pat vaguely remembered the sliding glass partition separating them from Roger.

On the way to the restaurant she rehearsed what she would say to Manheim. She felt terrible, on the tail end of the worst hangover she could remember. She promised herself she would stop drinking. Of course she would; she had willpower. She also had the craving for a Bloody Mary.

The car pulled to a halt outside Jasper's, a red brick town house with a tiny brass plate on a cherrywood door.

Before Roger opened the door, Pat popped four

Advil tablets into her mouth and swallowed. She got out of the car and, with some difficulty, made her way into the restaurant.

Manheim's thick body rose out of the semidarkness of the room as he lumbered over to greet her. The same beefy hand she remembered from last night guided her across the carpet to a table below a Turner reproduction of farmers tilling a field. Pat was thankful for the low light and murkiness of the place.

"How do you feel?" the senator asked.

"How am I supposed to feel?"

He laughed heartily. "So we're going to do that again."

"Do what again?" That uncomfortable feeling of having made a complete ass of herself last night started creeping in.

Manheim held his hands out in supplication. "Answering questions with questions. Bobbing, ducking, weaving. I felt I was in a prizefight rather than a conversation."

"My pugilistic counterpunching personality. My husband married me for it."

"How is Dr. Heller?"

"I'm not exactly sure. He's en route from New Mexico." She looked down at the silverware gleaming below her. "I don't mean to be coy, but what exactly happened last night?"

He leaned forward, elbows planted on the table, and stared at her from under his thick brows. "You were drunk but handling it fairly well. You told me what a son of a bitch and a bastard you thought I was. Accused me of things, some so clever I wished I actually had tried them. Unfortunately I am too shy and conservative. I appreciated your candor. Actually we had a ball. You honestly don't remember?"

Her eyes swept across the table. Wild thoughts whirled around her head, searching for a place to nest. "Only some of it," she said, knowing he knew that was a lie.

"You were very articulate, and to tell you the truth, I have rarely been interrogated by someone who had done such thorough research."

Had she pulled Kit Singleton's report out and hurled it at him? "I was hard on you because my readers deserve my very best."

Manheim responded with chitchat about life in the nation's capital, his plans and aspirations, what the state of Florida needed, and how he was going to secure it. Still worried about the night before, Pat knew he had wanted to meet her for some reason other than to provide her with a litany of "The Senator's Ambitions." She wondered what he had left out of last night's drunken exchange. Why would he want to have lunch with a reporter who so easily lost control?

After soup, salad and iced coffee she thought about ordering a glass of wine, but remembered her promise.

"Well," he said, "are you ready?"

"For what?"

"The guided tour?"

"Of . . . ?"

Manheim leaned across the table and folded his

hands. "Do you often have these blackouts? It's none of my business, but alcohol—"

"You're right, it's none of your business. You said something about a guided tour?"

"You insisted last night. I couldn't have gotten you in then. You refused to go back to your hotel if you didn't get a promise from me that I'd take you today."

She didn't want to hear about any more of the things she had done last night. It all sounded like someone else's life.

Outside as they waited for Roger to bring the car around, Pat put on her sunglasses, wishing she were back in her hotel room.

"Where are we going on this guided tour?" she asked.

"The perfect place for you to understand why the FDA should not limit genetic research."

Roger brought the car around, and Pat climbed in back next to the senator. After her performance last night, the least she could do was take Manheim's guided tour.

24

A HORSE BROKE OUT OF ITS STALL AND CRUSHED AMY, who flew up from the dust of the hoofbeats and into his arms. Josh could not hang on and dropped his daughter. Samantha suddenly materialized and picked her up. Samantha was taking Amy away from him. Pat was in the picture now, chasing after Samantha and battling for custody of Amy. Jim Ellison's big blond head loomed up. "C'mon, sleeping beauty," he said. "Time to rise and get with it."

In his haze, Josh mumbled, "Tell 'em I'm not here, honey," and turned over.

"Oh, so that's how you do it. Come on. Get your lazy ass out of bed. I got news, which I won't tell you unless you're standing in your own two shoes."

He heard a newspaper open and lips sucking in coffee and the sound of a cup plunked down on Formica. "All right," Josh said, "what's going on?"

"Your hearing musta gone during the night. When you are standing up, you get it."

"You know, Jim, no matter how wonderful you are with that terrific goddamn bedside manner of yours"—one foot was touching the floor—"even with all that, you irritate me sometimes. Not a lot but just enough to make me wonder why I ever"—both feet were on the floor, and both hands were beside his thighs—"decided to give you this much license to hand me shit that I obviously don't deserve." Standing, Josh shouted, "Now what the *hell* is the news!"

Jim was hidden behind the front page of the *St. Pete Herald,* one leg crossed over the other, laughing. Josh saw a hand appear and drag the coffee cup off the table and back behind the newsprint, and heard Jim's low growl, saying, "I found Amy."

"Where!" Josh yanked the paper away.

"I tracked down Samantha, who had taken her on a day trip to Disney World—no big deal. She wanted to explain the whole thing to you herself, but I told her you looked like a dead man and needed some sleep. I was going to drive you home, but you were such a slug—"

"Is Amy home? At Samantha's? Where?"

"At your neighbor's, Mrs. Plessey's, safe and sound."

"How long have you known about this?" At the sink Josh splashed water on his face. Without waiting for Jim's answer, he picked up the phone and called Jean's number.

Amy came on the line.

"Darling, are you all right?"

"Disney World."

"I know, but you're doing fine, huh?"

"Can we go back next week?"

She sounded as dopey as he felt. "You go on back to bed, baby, and I'll stop by later to see you, okay?"

"Okay, Daddy." Click.

Back to Jim, he said, "Any word from Pat?"

"Nothing."

One problem solved, another looming. He went down the hall and called Pat's Washington hotel. He left another message and then called Samantha, but her line was busy.

After showering and climbing back into his wrinkled clothes, he realized that Jim had not brought him up to date on the problems with his patients. When he got back to the office, his partner was gone.

Samantha's phone was still busy, so he decided to drive over to her place for some answers. Outside, the bay had a light chop and gleamed with sunlight, and the sky overhead was a deep cerulean blue, the color of Amy's eyes. The bridge was packed with traffic winding its way around detour signs. He passed the airport exit and turned right on Gandy, heading east around the bay toward Samantha's.

He was just groggy enough to forget the directions to her house, and for a half hour he drove around lost.

When he finally found the house, her Jag was not in front, and there was no garage window to peek through. When no one answered the door, he went around back to the pool. A green carpet of grass sloped down to the seawall and boat dock. The sliding glass doors at the back of the house were closed, the curtains drawn.

He discovered one of the kitchen doors was open. The kitchen was dark except for a red appliance beam and eerie white slivers of daylight on the porcelain.

He felt like a thief as he angled through the murkiness and flipped on a switch, flooding the rooms with light. Once again he could not get over the starkness of the place. There was not one personal thing—no photos, trinkets, or art objects.

He found the master suite. The bed was made and clothes hung in the closet like wooden soldiers, evenly spaced on identical hangers. Four dozen pairs of shoes were neatly arranged in a floor rack to anal compulsive perfection. He kept expecting Samantha to walk in any minute and catch him. He listened for sounds; he anticipated meeting someone around every corner. His pulse thumped, and his heart rate picked up considerably. In the bathroom he found makeup bottles and tubes stationed side by side; one toothbrush, one tube of toothpaste, one comb, one hand mirror, one brush, all the same dull green.

As Josh picked his way through the rest of the house he wondered what in the hell he was doing breaking into Samantha's house. He was a respected doctor in the community, and now he was a second-story man? He felt ashamed, and more nervous with every step that he took.

Finally he located Samantha's office. He found Adams Computer equipment, software, paper, invoices. He flipped through the invoice pages, rifled through the files, trying to leave things the way he found them. In the file marked "M.D.'s" something caught his eye.

He didn't think he saw it right the first time, but when he looked again, there was Ted Tozian's name, and the names of half a dozen other doctors he had graduated with from medical school. Bill Toomey. Sid Warner. And the ones who had died: Dave Morris, Gene Yardley, Bart Miller. What were their names doing here? A chill drove itself through him as he read on.

According to the invoices, they had all been using the services and technology of Adams Computer. He thought he heard a noise in the other room, and he held his breath, waiting. Moments passed, until he realized it was probably the headache that had started pounding in his brain.

Below his med school buddies' names were dates and names, financial statements, family histories, patient lists, income and credit reports, lists of friends' names, club memberships, medical and psychological profiles, more data on home life, strengths of character and weaknesses, hobbies, vices.

What was going on here, he wondered, with this woman and her inexpensive equipment? His own name appeared with private information that he thought only his broker or his lawyer was supposed to know.

His stomach burned when he thought about the mysterious deaths of his colleagues. Samantha had extensive files on all of them. Why?

And where did he fit in? Where was he on this hit list?

"Disney World," Amy mumbled in her sleep. The light was sharp in her eyes, and she turned away from it.

"It's Daddy, darling," Josh said, tears welling up in his eyes at the sight of his baby.

"Daddy!" Amy threw her arms out from under the covers and yanked him down to her. "Daddy!"

"You little strange wonder of the world, where have you been? It's so good to see you safe and sound."

"It's been nerve-racking, Daddy," Amy said, trying to sound very grown up. He loved her so much that sometimes it was almost too painful to bear.

"Well, I'm back and so are you, and I brought you a present from New Mexico." He pulled a red cowgirl shirt out from behind his back and handed it to her. She buried her face in it and peeked out at him from over the collar. "You know what this means, don'tcha?" she said.

"What?"

"That I'm an official wrangler, right?"

"That's you, baby."

Later that morning they sat across from each other at the breakfast table. Amy's pony stood out beyond the fence eating grass. The sun made a pattern of shadows on Amy's back.

"So," Josh said, now shaved and wearing old jeans and a faded denim shirt. "Did you have fun with Samantha?"

Amy made a face like a baby prizefighter and scooped a spoonful of cereal into her mouth. "She's not like anybody else I know, that's for sure."

"Yeah, how's that?"

"She asked me if I would like her to be my other mommy. I don't even know her."

Josh nodded. "What else?"

"Well, she certainly knows how to ride the rides in Disney World. She was very brave, Daddy. She didn't scream once, just sat there and gave me that weird smile of hers—you know which one I mean, when you smile but you don't really mean it. Like the one after you and Mom have a fight and you smile at each other like everything's just fine, but it isn't."

"Yes, I know the one."

"That's Samantha. And she also talks a lot, and you know what? I didn't know she knew Dr. Ellison that well."

"Dr. Ellison? How do you mean?"

"Well, for all the time they spent talking on the telephone she had to know him pretty well."

Samantha and Jim? "Do you remember what they said?"

"No, but it was the only time she got mad."

"Mad as in angry? She was angry?"

"Shouting. Or . . ." Amy looked out through the window. In her eyes he watched memories being sorted. "Tight-mouthed, you know? 'You do what I say and that's all I want to hear about it.'"

"Those were her words?"

"And how about 'We're on a timetable, my friend.' She said that one a lot."

186

Josh pushed his toast away and rested his elbows on the table, thinking about the files he had seen in Samantha's cabinet. And what did Jim have to do with all this? "Anything else?"

"I saw her going through the file cabinet in your room."

"You did, huh?" What exactly *was* going on here? "Anything else?"

"I can't remember, but she was always on the phone to Dr. Ellison and the other place."

"Which one is that, baby?"

"When she was sad."

"Go on."

"She kept apologizing and saying she was doing the best she could. She must have said she was sorry fifty times. I thought she was going to cry."

He pushed himself away from the table and took his dishes to the sink.

"Where's Mom?" Amy asked.

"Washington, D.C. She didn't call, did she?"

"We were in Disney World."

"I'm going to have to ask you to stay with Jean Plessey for a little while."

"I'm staying with you."

"There's nothing I'd like better, but your old dad has got some emergencies to take care of. When he comes back he'll take you anywhere you'd like to go. Busch Gardens? A movie?"

"So I guess I *do* have to go over to Mrs. Plessey's, huh?"

"How did **you get so smart** all of a sudden?"

Amy took **her dishes** to the sink. "I've been smart

187

for a while," she said archly. "You've just been too busy to notice."

"Well, aren't you the haughty one?"

"Whatever that means. Can I wear my cowboy shirt?"

"You betcha."

Amy threw her arms around her father and gave him a big hug. "I love you, Daddy."

"Just as much as I love you, honey."

"And you know what?" she said, walking away and stopping at the door. "I really wouldn't like Samantha to be my other mommy. Not one bit."

Josh was a half dozen blocks from Jim Ellison's house when he slowed the car down to a crawl. Kids played on the street in this neighborhood of large homes and snappy apartment complexes with names like the Bay Club and Turtle Island. Jim rented a comfortable two-bedroom house with all the amenities. The man stayed to himself; he was something of a recluse. Josh could remember visiting him only a couple of times in the two years he had lived here.

The house was stark, utilitarian, devoid of mementos, and Jim had done nothing to decorate the place. As far as Josh knew, Jim had no girlfriend and no buddies to speak of. Josh did not know why his partner refused to socialize. He and Pat had made every effort to invite him over, to include him in parties, outings, golf, but Jim almost always begged off.

Jim's house was a wide blue box on a smooth lawn

with clusters of palms symmetrically placed at either end, white-bordered windows and a brown front door. The house sat on a corner lot, closed off and characterless. If Josh were a thief he would not have bothered to rob it.

He rounded the corner and saw Samantha's Jaguar parked in Jim's driveway. Was there some secret liaison between these two? Josh felt a twinge of jealousy. Lonely man, lonely woman—what right did he have to object? More important, what about the hit list? Was Jim on it, too?

He parked two houses down and got out. The heat bore down as he walked across the lawn, his eye on the front door.

He hustled down the grass corridor separating Jim's house from the one next door. In Jim's backyard he saw a rusted swing set, sprinkler heads, patches of dry grass, a jalousied veranda, and a small oval pool with a self-propelled pool cleaner wading in stark blue water. Plastic deck chairs were neatly arranged around a wooden table.

He slid along the back wall listening for sounds, peeking through the jalousies' small glass roofs. He heard the metallic cadence of rock music from inside and then Jim's and Samantha's clear voices.

Samantha sounded angry. Josh heard her say, ". . . big trouble in Washington . . . not progressing on schedule."

Jim: "Whose fault is that?"

Samantha: "Not mine. *You* let him slip through."

Jim: "*You* let him slip through."

Samantha: "Where is he now?"

Jim: "He slept in the clinic and went home."

A pause.

Samantha: "I got a call from B., and he said to accelerate things. I have to go on to the next location, should have been there last week. But I had to allow for complications."

Jim: "You create your own. Your expectations have always been too high. Don't push so hard from now on."

Samantha: "Your Dr. Heller is particularly difficult. He will not budge like the others. But don't worry, I'll get to him."

Jim: "I hope so. Let me know. I've been ready with my part for three weeks now."

Through the window Josh saw Samantha standing over Jim, who was going through a file cabinet. He pulled out a folder and pointed to something. She looked at it, nodding her agreement. Their voices were hushed now, out of Josh's earshot.

Samantha took the folder and left the room, Jim followed close on her heels. Josh sidled along the wall, the rough surface brushed his shirt, his shoes scraped through the dry grass. Inside he watched their shadows moving toward the front of the house. Their voices rose and fell. Samantha barked orders, and Jim promised to obey them.

Josh stopped at the corner of the house by an oleander bush. He could not hear or see anything and debated going back around to the front and risk being seen. His problem was solved when Samantha walked out through the front door, saying over her shoulder, "Don't leave the office until you hear from me."

"Where'll you be?" Jim asked.

"Home."

When she had driven away, Josh went back around the house to the rear veranda. Five minutes passed, and Jim appeared in the living room in a beige suit and tie. Work clothes. He gulped down some juice, tucked a folder under his arm, and turned off the air conditioner.

Where was the connection between them and how far into the past had these two linked up? Who was B.? What had they meant about hurrying up the process? Josh needed answers. He watched Jim's Buick head off down the street, and he waited a couple of minutes before breaking the small window in the kitchen door, reaching inside to unlock it, and slipping through.

Josh went straight for the file cabinet in the back bedroom, moved the bookcase out of the way, and tried to yank open the top drawer. It was locked. He searched around the house for something to use, like a crowbar.

He found a lug wrench in the garage. He jammed the wrench into the edge of the drawer and pried. No luck. He was about to turn the cabinet over and try to bang a hole in it when he heard a door close.

Jesus. He pushed the file cabinet back into place, ran out into the hallway, and ducked into a hall closet that reeked of mothballs.

He heard footsteps coming down the hallway and

turning into one of the rooms. Another door banged shut, then what sounded like a dresser drawer. He listened to telephone buttons being punched and Jim's voice asking Julie if she had seen Josh.

"I was on my way in, but I forgot to do some paperwork, so if you hear from him, call me here. I'll be there in a couple of hours."

Josh felt around for the doorknob, found it, and turned. Through the crack he saw carpet, the wall, a baseboard. A wisp of cooler air hit his face.

He pushed until the crack was wide enough to slide through. He eased out, listening to the thumping at his ptemples. He was now out in the hall and moving toward the corner.

"What the hell!" he heard behind him. "Josh!"

His first thought was to run, but instead he turned around, caught. Jim looked from the open closet to Josh, and back. "What's going on, bud?"

"What's going on with you, Jim?" he said, taking the offensive. "That's what I want to know."

Jim took a step toward him and stopped. "I have a question. What the hell were you doing in my closet?"

"You want me to be honest?"

"No, I want you to unload a shit pile of lies on me."

"I want to know what's going on between you and Samantha. I saw her leave."

Jim dropped his eyes and tilted his head, calculating. "Going on?"

"You heard me. What the hell's going on between

you two? Samantha stayed with my daughter while I was gone, and Amy told me you two were acting real chummy on the phone to each other."

Jim let out a whoop. "You old dog," he said. "You aren't jealous or anything, are you?"

"That's—that's ridiculous," Josh stammered.

"She gets your dick hard, huh? I hope you don't feel unique in that. The male members of the entire hospital staff have been having better sex with their wives since she walked down the hall that first time. But, hey, you don't have to worry about me. We've been having loads of trouble with the new computer. Julie won't talk to the woman, for whatever reason, and you were out of town. Who else is going to be the go-between?" He stuck out his hand. "Peace?"

Josh took it. Jim grabbed his arm, spun him around, and slammed him against the wall.

Josh's face was pressed against the hard surface. He could feel Jim's breath against the back of his neck. "If you don't know anything, bud, what the fuck were you doing trying to bust open my file cabinet? Speak before I break your arm."

"Jim?"

"What?"

"Could you back off just a little bit? I can't even move my mouth." When he felt the pressure lessen and Jim's breath off his neck, Josh tensed his muscles and, just like in the movies, snapped his head back. He felt bone crunch. Jim let out a wail. Josh took the opportunity to free himself and run down the hall to the bedroom.

"You fucking son of a bitch!" he heard behind him.

In the bedroom Josh dropped to the floor and searched frantically for the lug wrench, figuring he had about two seconds.

He felt Jim's hands on his back, yanking him up. He spotted the wrench, grabbed it, and swung it high and wide, praying for contact.

He felt another crunch on bone. Jim released him, and when Josh turned, Jim was covering his face. Blood poured out of a wound near his ear. He staggered and pressed his hand to the wound. Blood seeped through his fingers. Josh pulled him down to the floor, face down, and yanked his hands behind his back. Josh used his own necktie to bind Jim's hands. Jim's nose had a deep bloody gash scaling the bridge; it was broken. "You going to tell me what's going on?" he said.

"Why'd you do this to me?" Jim said, wriggling his badly damaged nose.

Josh shrugged. "I once saw it done that way. Effective, huh?"

"You gonna fix my nose?"

"You talk, I fix."

Jim laughed through the blood running into his mouth. "Good luck. You're in big trouble, Josh. Too bad. I sort of liked you."

"Then I'll have to get Samantha to tell me."

Jim coughed blood all over Josh's shirt and face. "You're a lot safer with me. She'll mutilate you, that fragile young thing."

Josh left Jim there and walked out of the house. He

was haunted by what Jim had said: *"She'll mutilate you, that fragile young thing."*

Josh stumbled to his car, confused, fearful. His partner had tried to kill him. His friends were dying, and his patients were giving birth to red and green monsters. As he drove away, Josh tasted Jim's blood on his lips.

25

Pat spent twenty minutes driving through the city, listening to Manheim talking on the limousine's telephone. Then the senator ordered Roger to drive back to the Senate Office Building, where he had to "take care of a couple of things."

Pat waited another half hour outside the Senate Office Building. When Manheim returned, Pat smelled liquor on his breath. ". . . and then the prime minister leaned over to me and whispered in my ear, 'The only way to teach an old Banana Republic dog like that to sit up and beg is to start a revolution late at night while he's sleeping and feeling secure. Shocks the hell out of him. He gets the message real fast.'"

A real knee-slapper, thought Pat, studying Manheim's handsome profile and the road map of tiny red veins crisscrossing his cheeks. She looked at her notes and turned to him. "Is there anything you want to tell me about this tour?"

"What if I told you that genetic engineering is the single most important means of prolonging life and finding cures for incurable diseases? Researchers are hamstrung by government agencies that set progress back decades because of a bunch of slow-moving imbeciles on the government dole."

Pat watched his cheeks puff out and his lower lip rise out of a pout. His hands were red from nervous squeezing, and his foot tapped out a little rhythm on the floorboards. Manheim seemed uncharacteristically nervous.

The Virginia countryside was bright with wealth and breeding. White fences lined the road, and chesspiece handsome Morgans galloped across the gently sloping landscape. Big antique homes were set back from the roads behind oak clusters and tax shelters.

Manheim was circling *Post* and *Times* articles with a red Magic Marker.

They drove past red barns with white silos that looked like missile sites against the clear blue sky, through a town with shoppes, a ye olde inn, and an apothecary. Neighbors chatted in a post office parking lot filled with Wagoneers and assorted big cars. Up ahead was a wide gray and white archway with an elegant sign that read: DNA, Inc.

Pat looked at the sign and glanced quickly at Manheim, who stared straight ahead. She surreptitiously reached into her handbag and clicked on her tape recorder.

The limo made its way up a long winding road bordered by white-painted stones. The drive ended in front of a house with gables. Nearby she could see barns, fences, a circular drive and, out back, rolling acres.

So this, Pat thought, was where Manheim's money went. She noticed her hands shaking with anticipation and buried them in her lap.

A rigid little man with hair the color of rust and close-set eyes came out of the house and down the steps to greet them. The man, who was wearing a stained laboratory coat, was very intense and seemed angry. He was short and took tiny, delicate steps, as if picking his way rather than walking. Though he seemed quite friendly, Pat sensed a menace, a control, behind the veneer. She was immediately afraid of him. Manheim got out of the car to greet the man. After a moment he returned and opened the door.

"Pat," Manheim said, leading her out, "I would like you to meet the director of DNA, Dr. Bradley Burns. Brad, this is the woman I was telling you about. Pat Heller."

"The reporter who took you to task in Florida?" His voice was slow and measured and virtually unmodulated. He stared at her with fixed, unwavering eyes. He stuck out his hand. "Often these high-and-mighty guardians of the people, like the senator here, believe they're God-given rather than elected. They speak a coded language that says little but implies a lot. They use circles instead of straight lines to move from one place to another, and they're always looking over their shoulders rather than straight ahead. I am pleased to meet you, Mrs. Heller. Welcome to my little empire."

DNA, Inc.'s foyer and anteroom, both oak-paneled and elegant, opened onto gleaming corridors lined with offices, labs, animal pens. This was a model of organization and efficiency, costing, Pat estimated, tens of millions of dollars. All run by Dr. Brad Burns. They moved past a steel door that looked like a bank safe.

"What goes on behind this?" Pat asked.

"The future, my dear," Burns said.

"Then I would love to see it."

"In due time," he said. "The future must be doled out slowly if we are to comprehend its scope and not fear it."

"You've got my curiosity up so high that I won't be able to go another step without wondering about that door that looks so formidable."

"Therein lies the reason behind this company's existence."

"Then please, I would love to see it."

"You are a persuasive woman, and if I were a more flexible man I would fling open that door and show you, but I am not." When he smiled at her she noticed a proliferation of tiny scars—little patches of them, actually—spread over his face, as if some kind of surgery had been performed. "Not yet, anyway."

Burns continued. "My father was Dr. Bradley W. Burns the second." He led them through a hall that connected the main house to the laboratory buildings out back and then into a glass-enclosed atrium that caterpillared over a sloping lawn.

"The Chairman—that's what we called Father,

because he was on the board of so many corporations —had a vision of Mankind getting out of the rut of mortality. 'Why should we have to worry about when we're going to die,' I remember him saying, 'when we could put our energy into concentrating on how we could go on living?'

"His vision is now mine, and that is what we do here, Mrs. Heller. We dedicate ourselves to living as long and as well as we can. All things being equal, birth is not that extraordinary a process. We call it a miracle and romanticize birth. But the truth is, we know almost everything there is to know about birth. For me it's the prolongation of life that matters most. Conquering death is our concern at DNA, Inc. That sounds awfully melodramatic, and in fact it is.

"The truth is, the study of adulthood has got it all over the study of childhood. It's in adulthood that we do our thinking and build for the future, but not necessarily for our children. We build it for ourselves. And why not? We build it, we should enjoy it. All this about sacrificing ourselves for our children, for future generations! Are we sacrificial lambs put on earth to be drones for the queen bee of youth? If we build a house we should live in it. That's what the Chairman believed, and that's what I believe. In other words, our focus is shifting, and well it should. The indications are all around us. How often do we hear, 'I wouldn't bring a child into this overcrowded, anxiety-ridden world'? In the past we were pleased to bring in children, but no longer. My goal is to make this world a safer place to raise children. By concentrating on perfecting life, we'll eventually eliminate the fear of death." Burns smiled. "That is a flowery way of saying that I try to keep my mind on a healthy humanity."

They reached a two-story rotunda that surrounded an operating room with a small amphitheater filled with chairs for observers. A cadaverarium, Pat thought, remembering Josh's term for places like these.

"How do you finance all this?" she said, catching a look passing between Burns and Manheim.

"Contributions," said Burns.

"From whom?"

"Humanitarians."

"Politicians?" she said.

In the rotunda, lab technicians worked like little elves, busying themselves at their workbenches.

"Politicians like me?" Manheim said.

"It had crossed my mind." Again Pat saw Manheim glance at Brad, who shrugged.

"As a matter of fact," said Manheim, "I have made contributions in the name of science."

"Isn't there a conflict of interest here, especially when you're promoting a hands-off policy for the NIH and FDA?"

"I believe, as Dr. Burns does, that man should try everything in his power to prolong life. We should not be hamstrung by the snail's pace of government bureaucracy. My desire to streamline the bureaucracy is one of the chief reasons I joined the political process myself."

"To change it from inside?"

"You don't have to be so cynical, Mrs. Heller."

"It comes with the territory, Senator."

"There are still some of us who serve for altruistic reasons."

"And you're one of them?"

"I am."

She saw sincerity in his face.

"I am certainly not in politics for the money. Nor am I here for self-aggrandizement. Nor did I become a United States senator to overcome my shyness. I want to be able to go beyond limitations set by government agencies."

"So that what happened to your family won't happen to others?"

The shock of recognition registered on his face. "You've done your research. Yes. Precisely."

Burns said, "So now, Mrs. Heller, I shall tell you how I have tried to accomplish that here at DNA." He smiled through bone-white teeth. "Prepare yourself for an education."

Burns led her into one of the larger labs filled with computers and laboratory equipment, some of which Pat recognized from her research. It must have taken Manheim's millions, and more, to support an operation of this size.

"Can you see this?" Burns said, holding up a small glass cylinder. "Of course you can't. This is a gene extracted from a pregnant woman, and now . . ." He carried the cylinder to the largest of the machines and inserted it in a slot. "This is a DNA sequencer, a computer that analyzes all components of this cell, telling us its characteristics. In other words, the genetic code of the cell. Do you see?"

"So far."

"DNA is made up of billions of components. They look like little ladders. You've seen them, haven't you?"

"Yes."

"Only the lightning speed of this DNA sequencer can determine the cell's properties in a short period of time. Now, here," he added, leading them into another lab, "is where the real innovative work takes place—gene-splicing. We take the genetic makeup of the cell and splice in desired characteristics, then splice out those that are harmful or that we simply don't want. We don't want leukemia, so we remove the capacity for it. If we want larger breasts, we splice them in. I don't mean to be crude but this is how the process works."

"I see," Pat said.

"You want your child to be tall?" said Burns. "Perhaps one day you would like him to play professional basketball. There is no problem. You would like your son to kick sand in a bully's eyes. We can give him that capability here."

"You're able to do that, now?" Pat said.

"Big feet, healthy liver, giant sexual organs, if that's your preference. Long fingers for pianists and brain surgeons. If you don't want your children to inherit your congenital heart problems, it will be done."

"How long before you'll be able to do this with humans?" Pat asked.

"It's been going on for some time."

Manheim interrupted, "Well, not quite. This is

responsible genetic engineering we're talking about here, not some casual experimentation. Which is the way you've made it sound in your articles, Pat."

"With no legal constraints you could do whatever you please, on any human guinea pigs."

"Sometimes mistakes are made. Results aren't always what you anticipate," said Burns. Pat looked at his retreating back, wondering why he was being so candid about all this?

From down the hall Burns said, "I'll show you the special side effects chamber. It's behind the door you're so interested in."

This time Pat saw real panic in Manheim's eyes. He said to her, "Dr. Burns, like a lot of advanced scientists, is sometimes a bit graphic. So you must take what he says in context."

"What's in the special side effects chamber?" she asked.

"That's Dr. Burns's department," Manheim replied. Pat looked for evasiveness but didn't find it.

Manheim began walking after Burns, encouraging Pat to keep up with him. Pat was terrified. What did this half-mad scientist have in store for her? She kept the tape recorder going, just in case. She slipped out one tape and inserted another, burying the first one in the bottom of her handbag.

"What about growth hormone research and the like?" Pat asked Manheim as they hustled after Burns. "Any work on that?"

"Some."

"Can you be more specific?"

"Dr. Burns knows all about that."

"It seems as if you should know about it, Senator. You're turning Burns loose with a lot of money and a free hand. You don't know what he could be doing."

"I trust him."

"For all you know he could be shooting anything into these animals of his. What *about* human research?"

"There's always that need. After all, with advanced technology, we have to find out, after extensive animal testing, if humans could derive the same benefits."

"How extensive is this human testing?"

"I didn't say we were testing humans, just that it usually leads to that. Look at history. You'll have to ask Burns."

"He'll give me a straight answer?"

"Has he hedged so far?"

Burns entered the molecular biology lab. They found him at a chalkboard surrounded by charts and scale models of genes and cells.

"My intent," said Burns, holding up one of the models, "is to remove unwanted characteristics and predilections from the cell nucleus and to splice in more desirable traits. We perfect genes for desired characteristics outside the body and reinsert them via mouse viruses, or retroviruses. These viruses carry the new gene, alive and transformed, back into the expectant mother's egg, where they reproduce at an accelerated rate. We can target and modify genes for height, weight, heart disorder, precancerous growth, and so forth."

"You can take a cell from a pregnant woman,

redesign it, put it back in with these mouse viruses, and her child will come out whatever way you want?"

"Yes."

"Without her even knowing it?"

"Without her knowing."

"My God . . ." Pat gasped, thinking about the staggering implications of Burns's work.

Burns went on. "Molecular biologists insert the doctored section of the cell's nucleus into the new cell. The DNA ladders have what they call 'sticky ends,' which means that the new DNA automatically sticks to the old DNA."

Burns demonstrated the use of little pipettes in microscopic surgery to relocate the cells. "Rather simple procedure, putting the cell back inside the mother. A tiny injection, right there in the gynecologist's office, with the woman under mild sedation, if necessary. To get the cell back into the mother we have to use the specially altered mouse virus, a carrier molecule. This is where problems can come into play."

"Like what?"

"The genetic alteration is usually no problem. But the mouse virus can generate unwanted results when it comes into contact with the mother's immune system. Tumors can develop, cancerous and otherwise—large, often bloody festering tumors, rashes of them, that appear on the skin of the fetus."

"You can't get the altered gene back into the woman without these viruses?" Pat asked, her voice filled with panic.

"We've tried, but without the virus as transportation we don't have much luck."

"Then this operation could be done against the mother's will."

Burns's big smile showed over his small teeth and red gums. "She wouldn't have a clue."

"And you've done it?" Pat asked, terrified.

Brad Burns said nothing. Manheim, now extremely nervous, looked quickly from Brad to Pat. She had to get out of this lunatic's lab and back to the paper.

"We're going to perform an operation this afternoon, in fact." Burns reached up and took down a covered plastic dish. "You went to see Dr. Ellison the other day . . ." Burns said.

Pat gasped, and stared at Burns. How in the world did he know that, and what had Jim to do with Brad Burns or any of this? She felt as if a vise were tightening on her.

"And you felt a little pinch when your feet were up in the stirrups," Burns went on.

She felt numb, light-headed, and fought against the sensation.

"Here you are," Burns said, holding up the dish. "Your own little altered gene. I did the splicing on this one myself, knowing that you would be paying me a visit. And this afternoon"—he held the dish up for her inspection; the name running along the edge was Pat Heller—"I am going to reinsert it personally."

She let out a sound she could not remember having made before. "If this is some elaborate joke, I am not interested in hearing any more of it. I wish to leave."

"Of course," said Burns, "but first let me show you what's behind that door you were so curious about. The special side effects chamber. It's on our way out. We might as well take a peek."

As they moved down the corridor, Brad Burns said to her, "You see, this gene is just like Kelly Cox's doctored gene, which was recently inserted in your husband's office. And I've sent out new genes to dozens of other doctors throughout the country."

"My husband's patient Kelly Cox?" Pat said, stunned. She was having difficulty focusing on what was real and what was not.

"Think of it, Mrs. Heller: this is recombinant DNA of the highest order. I am able to code sections of the cell's nucleus to control sex, delivery time, and fetal development."

"What does my husband have to do with this?"

"Oh, quite a lot," he said, coming up on the door, "though he doesn't know it, and probably never will. These new 'Christmas babies' that your husband and the other ob-gyns are delivering are assured of certain physical characteristics and capabilities. They are the first proof of what we can do. My Christmas babies are a living testament to our years of tireless work. The Chairman died," he added. "But we've still got his legacy, his Christmas babies."

"That's a funny thing to call them," Pat said absently.

A tickle in Pat's throat suddenly erupted into a coughing spasm. Burns asked a security guard to fetch a glass of water. When he returned, he handed it to Pat who drank it down.

"Because I'm an egotist, or a signaturist. Now there's a word you probably didn't know existed until right now. You either, Curt."

Manheim was standing beside her. Pat tried to see him as her ally now, precarious as that tie seemed, against the raving Brad Burns.

"What's that, Brad?" Manheim said.

"A signaturist, leaving my imprint on the infants. Who among us has red hair and green eyes?"

"Red hair and green eyes?" Pat said, looking at Burns, barely able to concentrate. "Dr. Burns, you have red hair and green eyes."

"And what are the colors of Christmas, Mrs. Heller?"

"Well, of course, red and green."

"There you have it. When I send these small bundles out into the world they all have red hair and green eyes, my signature, or tattoo, if you will. Clever? Your husband hasn't told you that most of the babies born to his patients in the last few months have these characteristics?"

A chill shot through Pat. "He mentioned something . . ." My God, she thought, the genes, the cells. She was suddenly freezing, and she pulled her jacket closer around her. "It's time for me to go, gentlemen," she muttered. "Thank you for a very interesting tour." She turned and started for the door, feeling faint. She vaguely thought that something might have been in the water Burns had handed her to make her feel woozy. She saw up ahead two orderlies. Were they blocking her way? she wondered.

They entered a room with plants and trees and chairs lined up against one wall.

She heard Burns's voice behind her, saying, "Mrs. Heller, why don't you sit down, and we'll be with you in a moment."

"Well, I suppose I could," she said, and sat in a white wicker chair beside a ficus tree.

Pat watched Manheim take Burns aside and saw the two of them arguing about something. Their voices were almost out of range, but by listening hard and watching their mouths she could understand what they were saying.

Manheim: Why are you telling her all of this?

Burns: It's not often that I get the opportunity to explain to the general public what it is I am accomplishing here. It's a comfort to me.

Manheim: Do you know what she could do with this information?

Burns: Yes. Nothing. She's not leaving this building. I assume you have come to that conclusion by now.

Manheim: Yes, I suppose I have. This has gone far beyond—

Burns: Save the boyish naîveté for your constituency. I have not spent the last number of years waiting for one of your voters to walk in here and destroy my life's work.

Hearing "life's work" made Pat turn her head toward the door to Burns's special side effects chamber. She stood and had to hold on to the back of the chair for support. Something had definitely taken hold of her. Cautiously she moved toward the door, keeping an eye on the orderlies, who made no move to stop her. She pushed the door open.

Inside was a garden with light streaming down from the glass roof above. The room was filled with hundreds of trees, plants, and flowers. Two rows of glass compartments stood on either side of a center aisle. Music from the Italian Renaissance played in the background. The smell of roses and lilacs made Pat feel heady. Small tables and chairs reminded her of the café on M Street. Ahead was an alcove, a table with a salad plate, a bottle of wine, and three glasses.

She saw movement inside the glass compartments and went for a closer look. The creatures behind the glass looked like small animals, but they didn't move like small animals. She drew closer and saw that they were . . . children? "Oh, my God . . ." she said, trying to comprehend the horror that she could not believe was before her. Only in her wildest imagination could anything be this grotesque. Perhaps that was it!

She felt she must be hallucinating, no doubt from last night's drinking and this morning's hangover. The drinking and the hangovers for many months running. Was she having the D.T.'s? She knew it was time to quit. No more promises, she thought. She and liquor would take a long vacation from each other. Yet she was afraid to look back inside the cabinet. Her head pounded, her pulse raced. She could feel perspiration squeezing out of her pores.

Something touched her elbow and she jumped back. When she looked up, she found Manheim and Burns beside her.

"Please have some lunch," Manheim said.

"I'm not hungry," Pat replied, needing to rest as a wave of fatigue swept over her. Images of what she had seen inside the glass cubicles kept crawling up behind her eyes. "Could I lie down?"

"Of course," said Burns.

They led her to a chaise where she lay down before collapsing into sleep.

Pat awoke with a funny taste in her mouth, like chalk. She rose from the chaise and looked at the table. The salad plate and the bottle of wine were untouched. She wondered where Burns and Manheim had gone, but was actually glad to be rid of them.

As she looked around she remembered seeing something distasteful but could not remember what it had been.

The glass cubicles around her were dark except for a faint light that glowed from deep inside.

In one of them she saw what she thought was an animal of some kind—a pig? She had seen this before, she remembered, but where? What would a pig be doing here? Pat used her sleeve to rub the moisture away from the glass and peered inside. Then she rapped on the window. The creature stirred.

She rapped again and this time it dropped its feet off the bed and came toward her. A light snapped on, momentarily blinding her. When she got her vision back, she saw a very young child's face pressed against the glass pane of one of the compartments. It was a face disfigured by red marks and boils. The child's hands were also infected. She remembered Burns's descriptions of his experimental "things gone wrong." The child had red hair and green eyes.

Pat recoiled from the sight and turned away, only to see lights flicked on in the other compartments. She saw dozens of naked young children, all covered with sores, squirming in their glass cages.

She stumbled back to the center of the atrium, where she sat with her back to the children—the terrible consequences of Brad Burns's experiments. She heard voices crying, "Help meeee!"

She went to the door and banged on it until she had no more strength. She pressed her back against it and slid down to the floor.

Slowly the childrens' voices died out, the faces vanished from behind the glass partitions, and one by one the lights went out.

The door was cold against her back. "Don't sleep," she heard herself say out loud as she closed her eyes.

26

"JOSH, MY GOD. WHAT HAPPENED TO YOU?" SAMANTHA asked.

She led him across the gleaming floor of the living room to a sectional sofa and sat him down. "I'll get us a drink."

"Soda water for me," he said.

He watched her walk away into the kitchen and thought: This is a woman who knows all your medical school buddies, some of whom are now dead. She is in cahoots with your own partner in some plot. And she is out to ruin you in ways you don't even know about.

In a minute Samantha was back and sitting beside him. He drank the soda water and felt the cool roll of the liquid down his throat.

"Are you going to tell me what happened?" she said.

"I had a nosebleed," he lied.

"And?"

He heaved a beleaguered sigh. "I heard something."

"What?"

"It's stupid."

"Let me decide that," she said, giving him her best comforting smile.

"You and Jim Ellison," he said, watching her closely.

"Jim Ellison and I what?"

"Somebody at the hospital said she saw you two together. . . . This is stupid."

"No, it isn't." He felt her hands squeeze his as her perfume crawled over him. He knew she was putting on the charm, but he needed information. "You and he were seen being very intimate in the parking lot. There, isn't that stupid?"

She was undeniably relieved by Josh's story and smiled sympathetically. She reached for her drink. "When was this?"

"I don't know. Yesterday?"

She laughed offhandedly. "I ran into Jim in the parking lot. I had called him earlier about the computer setup, asked him if there had been any complications. You know how obsessive I am about doing well."

Josh said nothing, waiting.

"I stand very close to people when I talk to them, as I did with Jim in the parking lot. It's all sales technique. I nod my head a lot. Pretty soon the person I'm with starts nodding, too, and finally feels compelled to say yes." She gently raked his cheek with her fingernails. "You're almost ready to say yes, aren't you?" She sat back on the couch, crossing one leg over the other, exposing thigh to crotch.

"Josh," she said.

"What?"

"I have a confession to make."

He turned to face her.

"It's more of a request."

"I'm listening."

"I'm going away for a month at the end of next week, and I would like you to join me for a few days in the middle of it." She lowered her head and spoke so softly that he had to lean closer to hear her words. "This is the confession part. I think . . . I am falling in love with you. Don't say anything . . . not yet, please. I know this sounds absurd. We've known each other just a couple of weeks. I work on instinct, but it's all I have, and I feel this love for you." She wiped away a tear and stood up. "I'm sorry. This is not fair, to you or to me. If you want to leave, go ahead. I feel like a fool." She started to cry.

Josh took a handkerchief out of his pocket and handed it to her. She muttered a thank-you and wiped her eyes. He remembered the tough woman at Jim's and looked at this vulnerable girl crying beside him. He admitted he cared for her, in the way he cared for someone who needed help. Maybe she was being duped or was under someone's control. Maybe Jim was controlling her for reasons Josh had not been able to see. Maybe the hit list in her file cabinet belonged to someone who was exploiting her. But more than likely, he thought to himself, he had better take a look at the evidence, which indicated that Samantha was a hard-core manipulator who knew exactly what she wanted and would do anything to get it.

The telephone rang. Samantha excused herself and went into the other room. Josh crept to the door and listened.

"You do?" she was saying. "At the lab? I have no idea what he knows. . . . Brad, I'll do what I can . . . I'll call you in"—Josh saw her look up at the wall clock—"one hour. By then I should know whatever I need to. Is Manheim there with you?"

Josh blinked when he heard Manheim's name.

He heard nothing else of what she said. He started seeing connective tissue all over the place. Samantha knew Manheim, whom Pat was now visiting. Pat was obviously in danger. And who was Brad? Was he the B. they had been talking about at Jim's house?

Samantha walked back into the room and unfastened her sarong. "I'm going for a swim to cool off. Care to join me?" Without waiting for a reply, she slid open the glass doors and walked out to the pool.

He thought about her attaché case. He glanced quickly down the hallway to the office, wondering if he should grab the case and leave. Or maybe he should confront Samantha directly and get the answers straight from the source. He called Pat's hotel in Washington, but again, she was not in her room.

By the time he got outside, Samantha was swimming naked in the pool. He sat by the edge watching her gracefully slide through the water.

Samantha drifted over to the edge. "Come in. It's wonderful."

"I really can't. But about this thing with Jim . . ."

She waded away from him to the center of the pool. But she was back in a second. Suddenly her hands flew out of the water and grabbed him by the ankles. He toppled into the pool and started thrashing around. Water filled his mouth. His wet clothes hung heavily on him. Flailing, he grabbed the tiled border, gasping for air.

He searched for her, but she was nowhere in sight. Then she exploded out of the water like a dolphin and immediately plunged below again. He had an idea where she would surface, and there she was right below him, her hands crawling up his legs. He reached down, took her by the shoulders, and hauled her up. With one hand on the poolside and the other keeping her at arm's length, he said, "I'm very upset right now about a lot of things. Let's start with whatever's going on between you and Jim, then go on to my patient records and your extensive files on all my medical school classmates."

"I have no idea what you're talking about."

"I think you do."

"How would I?"

"I heard you on the phone just now. You mentioned Manheim, whom my wife is now seeing in Washington. I also know about you and Jim. I was over at his place before I came here." He looked for some reaction, saw none, and went on.

"You and Jim have been doing something with my friends, and possibly with my patients. I haven't figured that part of it out yet. Are you going to start talking to me?"

She pulled back from him, and he followed her. "I'm serious, Samantha. I need some answers."

"I tell you I love you, and you start throwing accusations at me. I don't know anything, but right now I'm not very pleased with you. I could have loved you, Josh, but now you're in the way."

"Either you begin answering my questions or I call the police."

She dodged and twisted out of his way, playing with him. Josh dog-paddled after her. Behind her he saw the gleaming metal of the diving board.

"Samantha."

"What, darling?" she said, leaning back against the side of the pool. "Tell me what you want."

"I want you to tell me where my wife is, why you have a list of my medical school buddies, why some of them are dead, and why I'm on the list. Start anywhere you like."

She smiled wickedly. "I promise to reveal all if you first come here and let me have my way with you." She gave a throaty laugh.

He kept his distance, trying to stay afloat, saying nothing.

She waited a moment. "You may or may not be pleased to know that you are the first man who has ever refused me."

"Give me a medal."

"I would love to, but it depends."

"On what?"

"How hard to get you play."

"I'm impossible to get. That should make it easy for you."

They were about three feet apart; at that distance Josh felt relatively safe. He wanted her to stay in the water because here at least she could not run.

She came at him suddenly and wrapped both legs around his waist. Like a vise, her legs began pulling him under. She pressed her pelvis against him. "You can't get away from me, you know."

Her lips were on him, teeth tearing flesh. He yelped and let go of the side of the pool. Her legs were fastened like suction cups, pulling him under the surface. She was trying to drown him. Water rushed into his mouth; chlorine stung his eyes.

He surfaced coughing and saw that she was hanging on to the diving board, her hands like hooks over the sides.

She readjusted her legs quickly so that they were clamped more tightly around his waist. This is it, he thought, she's taking me under for good.

He took a swing at her midsection and knocked the air out of her. Her grip loosened and then tightened again. He tried to land another punch by starting the arc below the surface, but the impact was lost.

Now he was underwater, his head pressed against her stomach, and he was almost out of air. His lungs were going to burst. He felt dizzy, light-headed; the energy drained out of his arms, then his legs. He felt the life seep out of him, and his eyes began to close.

Think, he said to himself. Think! He shook his head, searching for clarity. *Leverage.* The word popped out at him. He needed leverage of some kind. A foothold. He was facing the side of the pool.

Leverage! Lifting his tired legs, he pressed the soles of his feet against the side.

Then he ran his hands up along her thighs to her waist until he had a grip on it. His skull was ready to explode. He bent his knees and tested his legs.

Then, using his legs as springs, he pushed off the poolside, holding on to her waist, and up they went. A second later he felt contact above—as her head hit the metal board. Her leg-vise weakened, but she was not about to give up. She kicked, and he felt her grab his hair and pull. He seized one of her feet and bit down on it, tasting blood. She kicked and thrashed, but he would not let go of her.

He tried the poolside maneuver again. Legs bent, he pushed off the side. Another crunch and her legs unwound from his waist. He pushed once again, and once again he felt the jolt from above.

He was out of air and losing consciousness and knew that he had to get to the surface. Samantha was not resisting anymore; her legs floated free like lily pads. He pushed off one last time and broke the surface gasping for air.

His head throbbed. Blue sky broke over his eyes, and warm air blew across his face. He reached out and felt Samantha's lifeless body.

He saw a red liquid gash across the top of her skull, a crease with blood streaming out of it, mingling with the pool water. Her eyes were rolled back, her arms spread wide. Her mouth was open, frozen in a startled expression, as if she had been shocked to death.

He looked up and saw a stain on the underside of

the diving board—red blood smeared across silver metal.

He towed her to the shallow end and pulled her up the concrete steps and onto the patio, where he checked for a concussion.

"Come on, Samantha," he said aloud, "help me on this." His words sounded like a chant. Her pulse was gone; she wasn't breathing. In a moment he knew it was useless. There was nothing left to bring back to life.

Josh slumped beside her, exhausted and feeling the pain roll through him. Once his strength returned, he found a blanket to cover her and walked away, not wanting to face what he had done.

Inside the house he got out of his wet clothes and threw them in the dryer. He considered calling the police, but what good would it have done? First he had to find Pat.

In Samantha's back bedroom he found the attaché case, but no key. Taking the case with him, he went out to the car. He resisted the urge to rest or to think; he created a mental picture of Pat in his mind and focused on it.

Stay calm, he kept reminding himself as he put on the damp clothes and then left in search of a hardware store.

Josh drove around in a cloud. He saw a police car and was convinced that the officer was already on the lookout for the murderer of Samantha Adams.

At a hardware store in a mall he asked the woman

behind the counter if there was someone who could open his attaché case. She steered him to an old man with a white walrus mustache and beet red eyes, who seemed downright gleeful that he was asked to pick the lock. It took the man about three seconds.

In the parking lot, hands shaking, Josh rifled through the contents of the case.

The top folder read "Adams Computer Clients." It contained a list of names that matched the ones he had found in Samantha's file cabinet. The list included other ob-gyns he had been to school with, their patients, and many of his own patients who were due to give birth.

In the back of each individual file was a photo of the doctor with a woman standing beside him— Samantha, with her luxuriant shoulder-length red hair and piercing green eyes, wearing dark suits, looking very serious and businesslike.

He sat back. Five dead men, and another five on the list, including himself. Busy girl.

Josh came to his own file and read about everything he and Samantha had done, in detail: where they went, what they said, a progress report on their "relationship."

There was no mention of Jim Ellison anywhere. Had she been seducing him, too, in the event she couldn't get to Josh?

No wonder she had gone out of town so often. She had changed clothes, maybe even personalities, while visiting his medical school friends and having affairs with them. *I love you Josh, I am so lonely. . . .* He remembered Ted Tozian and the woman Barbara said was ruining their lives.

What in the hell was Samantha after with all this data on guys from his medical school? Was there a network of other Samanthas racing around the country, homing in on other obstetricians from other medical schools? To what purpose?

He needed answers. He ran down the list until he came to Rod Hardesty, who was at Ted's funeral.

According to Hardesty's file, Samantha had sold Adams equipment to Rod three months before and visited him on at least four occasions. Josh checked his watch; it was four o'clock in Minnesota, and Rod was probably still in the office.

Josh found a phone booth on the beach down near the Madeira bridge, under a sign, THE KIT KAT KLUB, a strip joint. The first call he made was to Pat's hotel in Washington, where he left another message. He then called Jean Plessey and talked with Amy, who said she had gone riding and was ready for bed.

Josh then rang Rod Hardesty's number and got his receptionist, who said the doctor would be with him shortly.

A few seconds later Rod's enthusiastic voice came over the line. "Josh, what the hell's going on, bud? It was good seeing you at Ted's. Jesus, what a string of bad luck, all the old guys going under. Don't tell me—you're calling from the morgue; they got you, too."

"Almost, Rod. Are you somewhere you can talk?"

"Yup. Fire away."

"I got some tough questions for you, so level with

me. Pat's life could be in jeopardy. Mine, too, and yours."

"Jesus, you've gotten melodramatic in the last coupla days."

"Adams Computer."

By the pause Josh knew he had struck home.

"What about it?" said Rod.

"Working good?"

"Sure, it had better be. I just bought it."

"The woman who sold it to you . . ."

"Uh-huh?"

"She's lying by her pool down here in Tampa, with her skull cracked open, dead."

Josh heard a sharp intake of breath. He could imagine Rod swiveling around in the chair, looking out through the window at Saint Paul's Cathedral on the hill.

"Miss Adams herself, Rod."

"Jesus."

"Here's the first tough question. Nobody on the other line?"

"Nope."

Josh had found a photograph of Samantha standing beside a smiling Rod Hardesty, with his arm around her. "According to this, the name she used with you was Susan Adams. Five-eight, red hair, green eyes, beautiful, lonely, on the road a lot. You didn't see much of her, but when you did it was—"

"That's enough. The answer is yes."

"I'm glad you're still alive, Rod. Which is more than I can say for five of our med school classmates who were apparently also in lust with Ms. Adams and who bought her equipment. She just about did me in this afternoon. She bashed her head on a diving board while she was trying to drown me."

"Oh, my God, Josh, she did? She's really dead?"

That was not exactly what he'd expected to hear from Rod, but considering how he himself had felt about her, he could understand the sentiment. "What I don't know, Rod, is why she was doing this. Was there anybody in it with her? How did you meet her in the first place?"

"A brochure was sent to the office. I was having trouble with my old system breaking down, and the price looked right. I got in over my head with her, Josh. Please don't say anything. Jennifer would—"

"Don't worry. So your own computer was screwing up. How?"

"Wrong data. Wrong entries. Incorrect diagnoses. It was crazy. My office manager went nuts. Happened all of a sudden, a goddamn mystery. To this day nobody knows what the hell happened."

Josh said, "Your partner . . . you have that young guy, what's his name?"

"Randy Devereau, helluva good doctor."

"Did he have anything to do with Susan Adams?"

"Not to my knowledge."

"How'd they get along together?"

"Cordial. Randy's a real loner, keeps to himself."

"No friends. Doesn't accept invitations. But great with patients."

"How'd you know?"

A herd of motorcycles roared by on the beach road

and pulled into the parking lot across the street from Josh.

"Apparently the partners we have are involved in this—screwing up the computers so that your Susan or my Samantha could set up her own data base. The partners were also doing other things I'm not certain about at this point."

"You're sure about this?" Rod said.

"I am," Josh said. "But why would she want to set up her computers exclusively with people from our medical school? I have the files in front of me, Rod, right out of her briefcase. She was after a group of us. Tozian was in love with a computer saleswoman, and most likely the others were, too. Do me a favor: call some of the other men in our class and see if they're going through this, too. I have to get to Washington to find Pat. Make the calls, get the poop, and I'll call you tomorrow sometime."

"Can you fax some of that stuff to me?"

"I'll do it right away. Be waiting for it, okay? And for safety sake, don't tell anybody, especially Devereau, all right?"

"You bet. Be careful, bud."

Josh thought about all the women who had given birth to deformed babies or who had died on the table for no reason. Back in the car, Josh sat behind the wheel and stared out through the window at the biker gang in the parking lot. What could a group of obstetricians out of the same medical school class have that someone would go to such extraordinary lengths to get?

He kept returning to his own computer screwups, the scrambled data. Rod's computers had broken down in much the same way his had. Could Julie have had anything to do with all this? It seemed impossible. Jim? What exactly was the connection between Samantha and Jim Ellison? Why was there no mention of him in any of the files when they had seemed so familiar with each other?

"I got a call from B." Brad.

"There's big trouble in Washington." Pat.

He started the engine and was about to pull away from the Kit Kat Klub parking lot when another thought struck him. He shut off the engine, got out, went back through the blast-furnace heat to the phone booth, and called Ted Tozian's office. His nurse, Wally Lopez, answered. He asked her if Ted had any trouble with computers a few weeks back.

"I almost went crazy," she said in her thick, smoky voice. "Ted started screaming at me for screwing things up, for ruining his practice. Then he calmed down, especially when the computer lady came by. He was very happy after that."

"What exactly went wrong with the machine?"

She gave him a litany of problems that was identical to Rod's.

"And how did you find out about Adams Computer?"

"Ted's partner, Dr. Wilkes, had a brochure they sent him, and the price was right. That's when the real trouble began, if you know what I mean."

"Is Dr. Wilkes there now?"

"He's at home. Would you like his number?"

"Please."

Wilkes sounded half dead when he answered the phone. He whined his way through the first few minutes, trying to answer questions about Ted having trouble with his memory. He sounded even crazier than he had when Josh saw him at Barbara Tozian's after the funeral.

"And how well did you know this woman?" Josh asked him, referring to Samantha, who had used "Sandra" with Ted's office.

"Know her?"

"Yeah, Rex, you know, as in what kind of a relationship did you have with her?"

"What are you talking about? Are you accusing me of something?"

"No, I'm asking you a simple question. You showed Ted the Adams Computer brochure, right?"

"How did you know about that?"

"I'm going to level with you, Rex. The woman you know as Sandra Adams is dead. She split her skull on a diving board not five miles from here. She had been using different names around the country, in doctors' offices—doctors I went to school with—and five of them, including Ted Tozian, are dead. She had something to do with their death, and I'm trying to find out what. Are you going to help me or not?"

After a long pause, Josh said, "Rex? I'm here and I need some help with this."

"We have to meet."

"Where?"

229

"Anywhere. I can't stand this anymore. I have got to talk to somebody before I lose my mind. Honestly, I am on the verge of a nervous breakdown."

"What about Washington, D.C.?" Josh said. "My wife went there to meet with Senator Curt Manheim, who may or may not have something to do with all this."

"Oh, my Lord."

"What?"

"All right, then, I know where we can meet. And we have to do it soon."

"Tomorrow soon enough?" Josh asked.

"Meet me at DNA, Inc., headquarters, in McLean, Virginia, just a few miles outside of Washington."

"I know where McLean is. DNA, Inc.? You have an address?"

"Four-oh-four Border Lane," Wilkes said. "There's a farmhouse down the road, red and white silo and an empty barn. Number one-twenty. Let's meet behind the barn, say . . . five o'clock tomorrow morning."

"Five in the morning?"

"Security is lax; it's a safe time."

"Can you tell me why DNA?"

"Your wife is there."

"She is? How do you know?"

"I'll explain everything when I see you."

"Rex, I don't have to tell you that I expect you to be alone, no surprises."

"Believe me when I say I want this cleared up as much as you do. You don't know how much."

Josh hung up and stood under the stripper sign. The sun beat down on him, and the waters of the bay kicked up oil from the tanker gliding by a few hundred yards out to sea.

Was Rex Wilkes on the level? No matter, he had to trust him.

He called Julie and told her where he was going to be. "If you don't hear from me by noon tomorrow, call the police and tell them where I am. If they don't believe you, tell them they can find the body of Samantha Adams beside her pool. And that I did it—in self-defense."

"You . . . killed her?"

"More or less . . . yeah, I did."

27

She opened one eyelid, then the other. A cool breeze brushed against her face and through her hair. The air seemed to come from everywhere, all at once, as if she were at the beach. The place was very comfortable, wherever she was. She didn't want to know. As soon as the fuzz cleared away, Pat remembered the glass cages and the children. She snapped her eyes shut against the image, but in the darkness the vision was even more acute.

She heard sounds of the sea and birds squawking and the tumble of waves. She imagined a lagoon and thatched huts with young men in longboats rowing out to sea over sun-dappled blue water.

The room was filled with bright light, as if she were outdoors. Now she saw a wicker chair and next to it a mirror with a bamboo frame, a brown wooden floor, an off-white wall. She felt no urge for a drink of water, which was unusual, for in the last few months every morning when she woke in the throes of dehydration she gulped down several glasses.

This morning she had no hangover, no headache, no cotton mouth. She heard hollow voices engaged in earnest conversation. One accent sounded vaguely Asian. She pushed herself up on one elbow and looked around her tiny cubicle. On the dresser was a tray with breakfast, the *Washington Post,* and a note.

The note read: "Make yourself comfortable. We'll be in to see you soon." It was signed by Brad Burns, Curt Manheim, and Faubus Leung. The welcoming committee. Pat saw the three of them standing out in the corridor and remembered the conversation between Manheim and Burns regarding her fate.

A *Post* headline told Pat that Manheim was slated to speak on the Senate floor tomorrow afternoon in support of genetic research and in the name of humanity's better health. If only his colleagues could see the results of that research here at DNA, Inc., she thought, knowing that she had to keep a cool head during her attempt to get out of this place.

Someone had mercifully pulled the draperies across the windows separating Pat from her deformed infant neighbors. She changed into her cleaned and pressed clothes and went out to meet her captors.

The doctors and the senator were in the midst of an argument. Pat heard accusations hurled back and forth between Burns and Manheim, with Leung's tranquil voice interrupting occasionally. She heard Burns telling Manheim to keep his speech simple on the Senate floor and to let nothing questionable slip. Manheim pointed out that he hadn't gotten where he was by making mistakes like that. Leung reminded them that rancor often led to the door of chaos.

"Mrs. Heller," Manheim said, noticing her arrival.

She looked from one to the other. "I'd like to go now before people start missing me."

Burns turned to face her. "Why? You've just arrived."

"You can't hold me here against my will," she said, thinking how ridiculous that sounded.

Burns smirked. "We can't let you leave except by the back door, and you know what that means."

"Dr. Leung," Pat said, approaching him. "It's obvious that Dr. Burns is not going to help me. Perhaps you'll understand. My newspaper editor, Bill Walters, is a very good friend of Senator Manheim. Bill knows I'm here interviewing the senator. He's probably already made a number of inquiries."

Manheim interrupted, "No calls, no inquiries."

"There will be, you can bet on it."

"We met for lunch, and you went on your way."

"You can't be serious," she said. "You simply cannot hold me here."

"If you were in our position, Mrs. Heller, knowing what you know," Manheim said, "would you consider release? Be reasonable."

"We're waiting for a phone call," said Burns, "and when we get it we'll decide exactly what we'll do."

"What phone call?"

"Informing us about your husband."

She could feel sweat gathering in her armpits. "What about him?"

"If he's alive or dead."

Her words caught in her throat.

"Somebody's already supposed to have taken care of him," Burns said. "I don't know what the holdup is."

"Who?" Pat asked. She felt sick, wanted to sit down.

"Somebody you know—Samantha Adams."

"We've never met formally."

"It's a long, fascinating story, which I'd be happy to tell you, but for now . . ." Burns sighed. "Let's just wait here quietly."

"My husband is not an easy man to put down, Dr. Burns. Maybe your friend wasn't able to do the job." Pat desperately hoped what she said was true.

Brad Burns screamed, "Shut her up" to nobody in particular.

"Nervous, Dr. Burns? Worried your grand plan might get derailed?"

With amazing speed, Burns reached over and slapped her hard across the face. She reeled back and swung her handbag at him. Loaded down and heavy, it caught the side of his head. He staggered back, and blood squirted out of a cut next to his ear.

"Get her out of here," he said in a low, tight voice. "Now."

Manheim took her arm and steered her toward the double doors.

"My husband will be here to finish you off," she screamed.

Burns laughed. "In a way I hope your husband does get here so I can show him what I'm going to do to you."

"You're the Christmas baby, Burns," Pat said. "You're the mutant in this crowd."

Burns composed himself and said with great calm, "Put her in number four."

An orderly clamped a hand over her mouth, then lifted her off the floor and carried her to the dark operating room at the end of the hall.

28

LIFE-AND-DEATH NOTIONS PLAGUED JOSH HELLER AS HE traveled to Washington, D.C., got a room for the night, and at three-thirty the next morning drove a rental car toward McLean. He thought about lost opportunities, shadow dreams, a missing wife, and a murdered woman.

In the moonlight the spot where he was to meet Rex Wilkes was not that difficult to find—the farmhouse, the red and white silo, and the empty barn. Unwilling to take any chances, Josh parked down the road behind a clump of bushes and angled around toward the barn.

It was just after 4:00 A.M. when he came through high grass and oak trees to the crest of a hill. On this crystal-clear night he was able to see down through the fields to a small lake nestled among trees. Cows and sheep grazed nearby, and he could see a wooden diving platform floating in the middle of the lake. He sat on the knoll and stared at this idyllic setting and thought about Samantha floating in the bloody water of her pool. It made him sick to think about what he had done to her, what *she* had done to his friends.

All trails had led him here. He thought about Pat behind the DNA gate. She was just minutes away, just over the ridge. His watch read 4:30. He left the knoll and walked to the farmhouse. There were no signs of life out behind the house or through the windows. No gardens grew, no chimes sounded, no voices, no farm animals. The grass needed mowing. No cars or trucks were in the driveway. The barn doors were closed.

He decided to get a closer look and moved diagonally across the backyard to the house itself. He looked through the windows where small night-lights illuminated certain areas. This was not an abandoned farmhouse at all but a wonderland of antiques and tapestries, wagon wheels, leather-bound books, and old paintings.

He saw a Burns coat of arms over the mantel, and a fieldstone fireplace. A short red-haired man in a jacket and tie sat in a leather high-backed chair reading a book.

Josh left the window and slipped along the side of the house, keeping the barn in sight, until he finally reached the driveway. Across the drive to the barn was a ten-second dash.

He had taken just a few steps toward the barn when he heard a car engine and saw headlights coming up the driveway. His adrenaline pushed him across the lawn and straight into a man standing in the shadows.

Josh rolled out of the man's way and went sprawling into a bush. When he looked up, he saw two maniacal eyes belonging to Rex Wilkes, who had one finger raised to his lips and one hand outstretched to haul him off the ground.

Once back on his feet, Rex led Josh around to the rear of the barn where Josh said, "There's someone living in that house."

"Of course. It belongs to Dr. Burns, who runs DNA, Inc."

"Thanks for telling me. You said it was empty."

"The barn, Dr. Heller," Wilkes said in his bland, uninflected voice, which sounded remarkably like Jim Ellison's, "I said the *barn* was empty."

Josh looked into Wilkes's bloated face, with the strands of blond hair flying about in the wind, and the crazed blue eyes.

"So," Josh said in a low voice, "what next?"

"We better get into DNA to retrieve your wife."

"What's going on here, Wilkes?" Josh said. "How did Pat get here?"

"If you follow my instructions . . ." he said, leading Josh into the barn.

"First let me tell you how I got here," Wilkes said. "In the best Dickensian tradition, they plucked me, Jim Ellison, and a number of other promising young boys from foster homes around the D.C. area—'they' being Dr. Burns's father and Dr. Faubus Leung, his associate. The two men educated us, sent us through medical school, and basically brainwashed us into believing that we were put on earth to carry out their mission."

"Which was?" said Josh.

"To enhance the quality of life through genetic research."

"Which included murdering my friends? What happened to Morris, Tozian, and the others?"

"We were required to do certain things. . . ." Wilkes slumped back against a stack of baled hay. "Twenty of us, including Jim Ellison and others, were assigned to doctors with established practices. We had orders to take over those practices at certain specified times during the last few months."

"Take over? How were you supposed to take over?"

"Once you and the others were out of the way, we would buy the practices and go on."

"With Samantha and her cost-effective computers."

"She was brought in to organize all the data. Her computers were on line with Burns's mainframe here at DNA, Inc. Samantha belonged to Burns's father. She was his . . . shall we say, creation?"

"Creation?"

"Young Dr. Burns said she was the only one of his dad's people who ever made it through the gene-splicing process."

Josh tried to focus. "Gene-splicing. You mean she's a test-tube baby?"

"The rather perfect test-tube baby, a masterpiece of perfect genetic makeup. She could have lived to God only knows what age if you hadn't done her in."

While Josh let that sink in, Wilkes went on.

"Burns's plan was to spend a few years preparing while he and Leung finished their experimentation.

They knew that only as ob-gyns would we be able to implant their new cells in pregnant women with relative ease. That's the goal of their research—planting perfect cells in unborn babies, creating a generation of disease-free, genetically improved children to inherit the earth."

An army of genetically engineered people with red hair and green eyes. "What about all the complications and deformed births? And the deaths?"

Wilkes shrugged. "Things went awry. Burns thought he had everything down pat, but obviously he didn't. Something was wrong with the viruses he used to carry the genes. He'll explain that to you."

"Why did he choose members of my medical school class, or were there others?"

"That you'll have to ask him, too."

A sliver of morning light appeared under the barn doors. The air smelled of hay, chickens, and manure. Outside a heavy dew lay on the trees, and the air was so thick with moisture he could have rubbed it between his fingers.

The whine of a car engine startled Josh. He looked to Wilkes, who said, "That's Burns getting into Dr. Leung's car. He picks him up for work every morning at this time."

Josh heard the grinding of gears and the roll of rubber tires over damp gravel.

Wilkes stretched and wrapped his coat around his fleshy shoulders. "I don't have to tell you how sorry I am this happened. I couldn't live with myself after

241

Ted, after I was ordered by Dr. Burns to . . . put him to rest."

"You killed him?"

"Let's say I orchestrated it, as I had been commanded to do. But the guilt afterward, the remorse . . . I haven't been the same since. That's why I said what I did in New Mexico, why I'm here with you now. I have got to stop this from going any further." His face looked pathetic, as if he had just discovered something truly loathsome about himself. "I guess they forgot to program the morality out of me." Wilkes laughed bitterly.

"But Samantha . . . I guess they got rid of hers entirely."

"A cold fish, that one. Classic anal retentive. Type A personality. Achievement oriented. Relentless. No sense of humor. I don't think she had one honest feeling in her, not one. Everything she did she did to get something. She lived by the strictest reward system I've ever seen. Spooky." Wilkes checked his watch. "It's time to go."

They left the barn and walked through the meadows to where Josh had parked the car.

"How is Manheim connected to all this?" he said as they reached the foot of the hill.

"I don't know anything about that."

Wilkes, as one of the brainwashed, seemed to have been given information on a need-to-know basis only. And Wilkes had no curiosity about anything other than what he was supposed to know about his mission. Burns and Leung had factored out inquisitiveness. Wilkes was brain-dead to anything outside his tight little world—except, it seemed, his guilt over killing Ted.

"Here's my car," Wilkes said.

"Mine's up the road a bit," he said.

"We can get it later. This will probably work better if we go in together."

They drove down Border Lane until they found the small elegant sign, DNA, Inc., and drove through the gate. Birds chirped. A red fox ran across the road. Josh saw the proud heads of deer in a field. The distance between the gate and the manor house on the hill was a half mile or so. "How do you plan to pull this off?" Josh asked on the way up.

"Walk right through the door."

He glanced at Wilkes, who was grinning and bobbing his head to some strange beat of his own. "Just like that?"

"They know me, and you're my colleague. Piece of cake."

"You're sure this is a good time of day to go in?"

"As I told you, security is light. If we have any problems, breaking out will be a lot easier."

"Breaking out?" That didn't sound at all encouraging. "What do you mean, breaking out?"

"I always look at contingencies," Wilkes said, bobbing, smiling.

"Do they know you're coming?"

"More or less." His head jutted forward. "Here we are. Don't say anything. I'll do the talking. But don't worry; we'll get these bastards."

"Look, Wilkes, this is not a commando raid we're on here . . . right?"

"Unlikely."

Josh watched the young doctor climb out of the car and start up the hill toward the Georgian pilasters. Josh followed. Mental alarms clanged all around him, tripping his instincts.

29

THE TINY FISH FLOATED IN THE WATER, ITS EYES BULGING. It lay on its side, small conelike mouth agape. Colored spires rose up from the artificial ocean floor where pebbles sat in an ornamental array, like gravestones. A shipwrecked vessel lay on its side while plastic mermaids danced on the blue sand around the sunken craft. A narrow tube rose up from the bottom of the tank, and a trickle of tiny oxygen bubbles flowed from its nipple.

Curt Manheim stood over the aquarium, a gift from his daughter long ago—the week before she died. "I couldn't have helped you then," he muttered, feeling the tears forming.

The pain was too great for him to dwell on, and he turned his attention to the dead fish. Obviously the tank's mechanism had failed. The fish's life-support system had given out, just like his daughter's.

It was six in the morning, and he was in the Senate

Office Building, without having slept. He had stayed awake all night, wishing he had never gotten involved with Brad Burns and Faubus Leung.

The speech he was to deliver on the Senate floor this afternoon was on his desk. He knew it by heart; he had been practicing it for ten years. He had the support of a small majority of his colleagues, but the vote was going to be close. There was growing dissent over government control of research projects, and people were distressed because the slogging bureaucratic leviathan was falling behind their demands. Protests rose over certain foreign drugs that were banned in this country, along with objections from the scientific community that researchers abroad were winning all the prizes and big-money grants.

Manheim had gathered the support of eminent scientists from government and the private sector, top-of-the-line academics and big drug company CEOs.

But was this the way to go about it? A moral twinge had been insinuating itself into his daily thoughts. Brad Burns had said, "You think too much. Just do what you're supposed to." Normally a healthy piece of advice, but when Manheim thought about the experimental children in Burns's glass houses, he wasn't sure anymore.

The senator glanced out the window at the sun rising over the trees. He lifted the fish out of the water and stared down into its ugly dead eyes.

A tear fell out of his own eye and splattered on the fish. His hands shook, and the fish squirted out of his hands. He looked down at his palms and rubbed them together. He took a handkerchief out of his pants pocket and wiped them dry.

Soaked with perspiration, he made his way back to his chair, supporting himself along the edge of the desk as he moved. He eased himself into the chair and leaned back in its contours.

The fish was lying somewhere on his floor—like the senator, it was dead but not buried.

30

SHE WAS TIED TO A ROTATING SPIT. IN FRONT OF HER, HER husband and daughter were singing a song she could barely hear. The song was about her. They were pointing at her, their laughter full of ridicule. Bill Walters, Brad Burns, and Curt Manheim were with them, aiming their fingers at her.

Each time the spit rotated, her mouth was forced open and gin was poured down her throat. She gagged on the gin, spit it out, and then threw up as she continued to rotate on the spit. The laughter grew louder as she turned faster and more gin was poured.

She could barely breathe, and as she spun faster the faces became a blur. The gin bottle began hitting her in the head, and she was drowning. Gagging, sputtering, she knew she was going to die.

Pat Heller bolted straight up in bed. The nightmare was all around her. She could not bear to open her eyes for fear of what she would see—her "roommates," as Burns called the children in the adjoining cubicles. For the last ten hours she had been with them, listening to their muffled cries.

She alternately feared and sympathized with them. She could see the sadness in their eyes, and the pain. Their cries came from deep within, from the terrible knowledge that they would die soon because their bodies' immune systems could no longer fight the cancerous tumors sprouting out of them.

She turned over and shut her eyes, but sleep wouldn't come. The fear that she, too, might never get out from behind these glass walls kept her awake.

Brad Burns tugged at his earlobe, rubbed his eye, and looked through a pipette at the liquid he had taken from one of Dr. Faubus Leung's incubators.

"So this is it?" he said to Leung, who stood like a statue in an Oriental garden. "That's what you said the last ten times."

"I am certain," Leung said in his soft, unmodulated voice.

"I understand the implications, but what is to prevent the mother from contracting tumors, just like the baby? Then there's the question of what happens to the baby while it's alive in the mother's womb. The disease would spread, would it not?"

"It didn't spread in the animals we tested."

Burns knew if this particular isolated gene worked, the floodgates of genetic research would open. He would be able to screen the DNA of patients to identify neurofibromatosis, for instance, by the appearance of dark patches on the skin, called café-au-lait spots. It was all in the isolation of genes. In the last few years he had been able to isolate genes that caused cystic fibrosis, Duchenne muscular dystrophy, colon cancer. He would be able to isolate and remove these genes during the initial stage of pregnancy, banishing them from children forever.

The only significant problem at this point, aside from introducing the altered gene into the cells, was the altered virus used as the carrier molecule.

Burns walked away from the pipette, his soiled medical whites flapping behind him. He hadn't slept in a couple of days, mostly from fretting about Manheim and his speech to the Senate today. He also wondered what he was going to do with Pat Heller. The problem wasn't actually what he was going to do with her—he knew that—but how to steer inquisitive people in other directions if they came looking for her.

There were too many problems all of a sudden. He needed a rest. "Faubus?"

"Yes."

"We have children here we can test this on. We may as well give it to them and record the results. Can you set it up?"

"Immediately." Leung turned and started for the door.

"If it takes as little time as you say it does, we should be finished and on our way to breakfast in forty-five minutes."

"Or less," said Leung, going through the door.

Burns stared after the old man, who was at least seventy-five. He reminded Burns of one of those ancient T'ai Chi masters who gave demonstrations in front of New York City department stores like Macy's where the master would lie down on the sidewalk and hire motorcycles to run him over to show how strong he was.

Faubus Leung never complained and was confident about everything he did, even if it didn't work the first few times. Burns appreciated that about the man. Faubus was just like his daddy, God rest his soul. Daddy also never gave up. Faubus and his daddy had been partners for forty years. Brad missed his father. He sat down and stared out through the window at the beautiful country morning and thought about his father's dreams. Brad was on the verge of fulfilling the old man's aspirations.

"To you, Father," he muttered.

Josh did not like the way he felt as he and Dr. Rex Wilkes walked down the long corridor from the entrance to DNA, Inc. They were moving in the direction of a one-story laboratory building that stretched toward the back of the property.

He remembered what Wilkes had said about the young men recruited off D.C. streets, turned into doctors, and sent out to infiltrate established obstetrical practices with orders to eliminate the doctors and take over. All this evil work was aided and abetted by the red-haired, green-eyed harpy, Samantha Adams.

He had to get word to the authorities about this, but first he needed evidence. And Pat.

Up ahead he saw a man who looked very familiar. The small, hesitant steps he took jarred Josh's memory. He could not place the man's face, which was disfigured, possibly by fire.

Wilkes took him by the arm. "Dr. Burns, I'd like you to meet a colleague of mine, Dr., ah . . . Ripley, from Florida."

"Dr. Ripley . . . so nice to meet you. This is the ideal time to have a look at our facilities."

Burns detailed the marvelous things DNA, Inc., was preparing for humanity. Again, Josh fixed on the man; he knew this guy, but from where? The shock of red hair, the green eyes, the white, freckled skin. The arrogance was particularly familiar.

Closer to him now, Josh could better see the tiny facial scars. Burns had undergone extensive reconstructive surgery.

"Is anything the matter, Dr. Ripley?" said Burns.

"Beg your pardon?"

"Do I have food on my chin or something? The way you're looking at me makes me wonder if some of my breakfast didn't make it to my mouth."

"Sorry, I'm just a bit weary this morning."

"We'll make this as painless as possible. Why don't you come along with me?"

Burns took Josh through the labs, showing him the computers, the DNA sequencer, and the graphs that charted the work the company was doing. Nothing to suggest the kind of treachery Pat had suspected.

Burns led him to the rear of the laboratory area and into a light-filled atrium building with white wicker furniture and ficus trees. Josh noticed a couple of security guards stationed by the entrance; their dark uniforms stood in stark contrast to the brightness of the place.

Josh heard Italian Renaissance court music playing, just as he had at Samantha's. He caught sight of movement behind what appeared to be large glass cubicles lining the corridor.

The glass itself was pitted, but on closer inspection he saw that one shield of glass had been pulled across another in each of the cubicles, like sliding doors, and figures moved around inside.

"What's back there?" he said to Burns, who turned and smiled, his small teeth peeking out from under his lips.

"Patients," he said. "We have a limited number of special cases here at DNA. Would you like to see them?"

"I would," Josh answered.

Burns shot a quick look at Wilkes and then moved over to one of the glass cubicles. "Now, you have to realize," Burns said over his shoulder, "that what we have here is the result of experimentation. In the history of science and medicine there've been many bad turns and miscues. No pain, no gain, to borrow a contemporary axiom. You might want to step closer for a better look."

Josh approached with caution as if a bell had gone off signaling disaster behind the glass. Shafts of yellow light showering down from above gave the atrium a cathedral atmosphere. Burns pressed a small beige button, and the glass door began to slide back.

What Josh saw repelled him. Children, from infants

to five years, all of them pathetically diseased, with silver dollar–sized tumors covering their bodies. All had red hair and green eyes. Burns was now pushing other beige buttons, and other glass doors were opening.

"You might be interested in the specimen behind this door, Dr. Heller," Burns said. Josh immediately realized that Burns was not calling him Dr. Ripley anymore. He looked at Wilkes, who was staring at the experimental children.

The panel slid back and there, curled up in a fetal position on a hospital bed, was Pat. She held an arm up to shield her eyes from the blinding light. Josh banged on the glass, calling out her name.

"She can't hear you."

"Let her out of there."

"In good time." Burns sat on the edge of a small instrument table. "You don't remember me, do you?"

"Should I?"

"I have to admit that you were one of the more pleasant ones, but just the same you got your licks in."

"In what?"

Like a wand, Burns ran one hand across the contours of his face. "I'm one of my own best experiments, Dr. Heller. I used myself as a guinea pig. Things went awry, and I started looking like them"— he waved an arm in the direction of his experiments —"on a smaller scale because I took smaller dosages. Then I said to myself, Why should I experiment on myself when there are others who would serve the same purpose?"

"Thus the plastic surgery."

"I won't, sweetheart." *And I won't let Burns keep us here either,* he thought. Pretending to keep his eyes closed, he squinted to watch the guards and gauge the distance to the door.

"He's crazy," Pat whispered in his ear. "You should see what he's done."

"I have."

"He's not going to let us out of here."

"We'll see."

He felt her tense, as if what he said had given her hope.

"I adore reunions," Burns said. "Except that I never attended any official ones. I was too busy here trying to make things right in the world. It's all Darwinian. Very simple, very complex, like life itself, like the business we're in here at DNA, Inc., the pursuit of perfection."

"You call this perfection?" Josh said.

"The path to it. These children have made it possible for me to alter the DNA ladders in the cells I engineered in my lab, the cells Jim Ellison took from your pregnant patients and sent up here for analysis. For each cell sample he sent, Dr. Ellison received an entire new set of genetic characteristics. The mothers now have healthy, long-living, disease-free babies."

"Those who lived."

"Ah, yes. But in those that did—the absence of pain, the wonder of life, the immortality that will come to all of us soon enough. Do you think what these poor children sacrificed isn't appreciated? How many martyrs have made it possible for others to live? These are the saints of the world, Heller, watching you from inside their glass cells. They gave a great deal more to the world than you and your gynecologist chums ever will."

Josh released Pat and turned to Burns. "You don't give a damn about these children, do you? You can't have changed that much from med school, where you loved only one thing, yourself. Look at the destruction you caused there, and what you've done here. You've infected these children, killed off a half dozen of your classmates, and turned Jim Ellison and the others, including poor Rex here, into robots who'll do your evil bidding for you. To save mankind? Please, Brad, try to come up with a better one than that." Josh walked up to him and stopped just inches away.

"Your father bailed you out of med school. Actually, I heard he pulled strings to get you through. Who's going to do it now, Manheim? Give it up. I'll call the FDA and have them come down to get you before you hurt yourself."

He could see Burns's eyes starting to spin. The little guy was going off somewhere. Josh wasn't sure this was the way to do it, but he had only one objective, to get out.

"I remember the word around school about what your daddy said to the university president: 'I want Sonny to get his degree. I know he hasn't got it all upstairs, but let's talk turkey here. If you don't graduate him, I won't give you the two million for the new psycho wing.'"

Burns stopped shaking long enough to aim his finger at the two guards and say, "Get them out of here." One of them pinned Josh's arms behind his back while the other one took hold of Pat.

Burns reached into his pocket and took out a rectangular plastic container about six by two inches, which held a syringe. He held the syringe up to the light. Josh saw that it contained a fluid the color of urine. "I don't know exactly what this is going to do," Burns said, "but since I was going to test it on your wife anyway, we shall see."

He looked up at them. "I feel I should tell you what Dr. Leung said about this virus. He said it works rapidly and in unpredictable ways." He turned to Rex Wilkes, whose head bobbed furiously, and said to him, "Rex, does Doc Leung tend to exaggerate?"

"No," said Wilkes.

Burns, holding up the syringe, turned back to Pat and said, "Bon voyage, Mrs. Heller."

"No!" Wilkes cried out. "Don't do that."

Burns looked at him, irritated by the outburst. "Now, Wilkes, you stand your ground and be quiet."

He turned back to Pat and motioned for the guard to hold out her right arm. He started searching for a vein.

Wilkes let out another bloody cry and flew straight into Burns, who raised the syringe in defense, and they toppled to the floor.

The guards rushed over and tried to pull them apart. Josh could see Burns's arms wriggling under the length of Wilkes's body. He saw a spill of blood.

Wilkes screamed once more and then abruptly froze up. Moments later tiny red blotches began appearing on his body. Josh recognized them as similar to the ones on the children.

Josh took Pat by the arm and, keeping an eye on the scene, started backing toward the door. It wasn't until they were out of the atrium and heading down the hallway that they heard the alarm.

As an escape route the front entrance was out of the question, and the rear was a mystery. The windows were high up on the walls and out of reach. Pat hunted back through recent memory to the tour Burns and Manheim had given her, but could remember no specific exits. In which case they were doomed to roam these halls until they were caught and subjected to what they had just seen Rex Wilkes go through. The idea sent shudders through her; she would rather have died, and she decided that she was prepared to if faced with Burns's syringe.

Down the hallway they saw two white-coated orderlies and ducked through a door marked INCU. The room was filled with small beds with tubes hanging above them like ganglia, and control panels—a laboratory of some kind, for the "betterment of mankind." They moved through this room and into another. This one was dark and cavernous.

In the dim light they saw rows of bleachers and walkways like seats in a stadium or an amphitheater. As they moved forward around the perimeter they heard voices from below, in the center of the hall, in the pit. The voices belonged to women, and to young children. Josh could tell by the timbre of their voices that some were newly born.

"Can you see down there?" he whispered.

"No, and I don't think I want to." Pat recognized how young the voices sounded, too, and thought about the child she was carrying. Would it survive this? When would she tell Josh about it? The thought gave her strength to go on.

They saw an exit sign on the opposite side of the arena. This was their way out, but into what? Josh wondered. He took Pat's hand, and together they started forward in the dark. Just as they reached the door the overhead lights snapped on, flooding the arena with light.

Josh looked down past the rows of seats into the center of the arena where under a dome of glass he saw what looked like a makeshift delivery room, with maybe two dozen beds. The beds had babies in them; their mothers were breast-feeding them.

Pat dug her fingers into the railing. "Oh, my God . . ." she whispered.

All of the children had red hair and green eyes, and their bodies were covered with the same tumorlike sores.

The mothers had recoiled from the light but were now recovered and staring up at them, their eyes like massive saucers, deathlike in the silence. In their light blue smocks with bright yellow flowers, they looked more childlike than the children.

Josh heard footsteps and looked up to see two guards racing at them from the opposite side of the arena. He took Pat by the arm and led her out through the door. They found themselves in a laundry; then they passed through another door into an equipment room. Though they figured they were still on ground level, they had little idea where they were, probably moving in a circle and certain to be caught. The farther they got from the main road, the more distance they put between themselves and safety.

They heard the low whine of another alarm, voices behind them, and voices up ahead. Josh pushed open a door that read CELLREP and came upon two men in lab coats working at a table.

"Excuse me," he said cheerily. "Brad Burns told us to meet him on the back lawn or the side lawn. Could you direct us, please."

"Out this door," one of them said, pointing his finger. "Turn right and then left, and you'll be at the rear of the building. Side lawn or back lawn?"

"I get so furious with Brad sometimes," Pat said. "He always does this, as if we're supposed to *know.*"

The two lab men nodded to each other in agreement.

"And we are also developing a chill, my husband and I. Do you have coats we could wear until we find out where Brad put ours?"

"Of course."

The tall man with the Ichabod Crane face took two lab coats from the rack and handed them over. On her way out Pat slid a clipboard under her arm. In the corridor now, they walked briskly toward the exit, speaking in professional-sounding babble as they moved.

Ahead were double doors and, through the glass, a spread of lawn and trees beyond. Behind them they heard sentrylike steps marching on the linoleum.

The doors were locked, so Josh, holding his finger to

his lips to signal quiet, casually walked over to the lounge area for a chair. He carried the chair back and slammed it into the glass door. This set off yet another alarm. After kicking the jagged edges of glass out of the frame they stepped through to freedom. They hurried into the forest that surrounded the grounds, then started angling back toward the main road.

Behind them they heard shouts and a voice over a loudspeaker. Sun slanted through the trees, leaving patches of light on the hard brown earth. The shouting and the alarms faded, and they could hear only the internal rhythm of their breathing, and the wind.

Pat moved forward, her head throbbing from the ordeal in town with Manheim and the knockout drug she was sure Burns had given her. She wanted to die, but not until they reached safety.

By the sun's position Josh estimated that they were moving south toward the main road. Where they would meet it and how far they would have to go for help, he could only guess. He did not remember seeing many homes in this remote rural paradise.

"Pump your arms," Josh said over her shoulder. "Lift your chest."

She pumped her arms and lifted her chest.

Eventually they stopped to rest and flopped down on the ground under a cluster of oak trees. The sky was darker now with rain clouds. Pat lay with her head against his arm and closed her eyes. Josh could hear the rhythm of her breathing and smell the fragrance of her skin. "Now that we have a moment," she said, "how are you?"

"Never better, and you?"

263

She laughed. "And our darling daughter?"

"Getting fat at Jean Plessey's."

"And the inimitable Samantha Adams?"

He paused, then answered, "Dead."

He felt the jolt of her head rising up. "Dead?"

"I have a story to tell you."

"I'll bet you do."

Wild strands of her hair blew against his face; old memories of them hurried together through his mind. "I love you," he said.

"I would hope so, after all this."

The clouds burst open and dropped a heavy rain on them. Their clothes became drenched, and they slogged along directionless, searching for a two-lane blacktop road with a freshly painted yellow stripe down the center.

When they finally found the road they headed east through a tree line running parallel to it. Josh looked at his watch. It was 10:45 A.M. He kept a lookout for Brad Burns's silo and farmhouse, or the barn where he had met with the late Rex Wilkes. He trembled when he thought about him.

"Even though we look like a couple of drug-crazed middle-aged nomads," Pat said, "we could walk up one of these long driveways and ask for help."

They chose one that wound up from the main road through elms and sycamores. They had not gone more than fifty feet when they were met by an Oldsmobile station wagon. The driver, a stout woman of about forty, jammed on the brakes and rolled down her windows.

"I'll do this," Pat said, moving ahead of Josh to the

driver's side. She introduced herself and her physician husband, explaining that they had run out of gas and gotten caught in the storm. They were looking for the home of their dear old friend, Dr. Brad Burns, who lived around here somewhere. The woman offered to take them directly to Burns's house herself.

"We'd rather go into the village," Pat said. "For gas."

The woman asked a lot of questions about Brad Burns and DNA, Inc. Both, she said, were a source of curiosity in the neighborhood. After a few minutes on the road, they came upon three men. Josh saw immediately who they were and urged the woman to keep driving.

"Why, it's Dr. Burns," she said, putting her foot on the brake.

"Don't stop!" Josh cried out. The car swerved over to the side of the road and lurched along the shoulder until it finally plowed to a halt.

Burns and two guards were at the window. "Thank you," the red-haired doctor said to the woman. By this time the guards had the passenger door open and were pulling Josh and Pat out.

"Call the police," Josh shouted to the woman, who looked questioningly at Burns.

"Patients," he said confidentially to her. "Harmless. Delusionary. Keep it under your hat."

"Of course," she said.

"You've done an excellent service by bringing them to me. You're to be congratulated, Mrs. . . . ?"

"Broward. Elisa Broward. How do you do?"

"Much better now, Mrs. Broward. Thank you."

Burns waved to Mrs. Broward as she drove off and then joined Pat and Josh and their keepers by the DNA, Inc., sedan.

"Look at all the trouble you went to when all you had to do was take the direct route," Burns said from behind them. "What savage maneuverings we sometimes make."

"Mrs. Broward will think about what she saw," Pat said.

Burns laughed at that.

"She was very curious about what you do at DNA, and we told her just enough to bring her and the police back to visit you."

Brad walked up to Pat, stopping just inches from her. "Manheim was right. You *are* a problem."

Burns and his men loaded Pat and Josh into the sedan and drove them to the clearing where Josh had left his car. Once they were out of the car Josh got the message: the plan was to incapacitate the doctor and his wife and remove all evidence of them. One of the assistants would leave Josh's rental at the airport.

"This is the proverbial end of the line," Burns said to them. "I had thought I might be able to keep you around for observation. To see how you and the baby would be doing, Mrs. Heller."

Josh looked quickly at her and then at Burns.

"Is the baby a surprise?" Burns said to Josh. "What perfect timing. The irony of it all."

"I was going to tell you . . ." Pat said to Josh, her voice trailing off.

He put his arm around her and held her close.

Burns removed another of his oversized syringes

from his pocket and held it up for inspection. "I don't like to do this sort of thing away from the lab, but in your case . . . the liability is too great."

"How vigilant of you, Dr. Burns," Pat said sardonically.

"This is the same virus that didn't agree with Rex Wilkes, so you know it works mercifully fast. Just so you have an idea of what to expect."

"Not today, Sonny," Josh said and kicked out at him, catching him in the lower abdomen. Burns was more surprised than hurt.

"Take that thing away from him!" Pat shouted, which Josh took to mean the syringe.

He lunged for it, grabbing the little man's wrist.

But Burns was not about to let go. He squirmed around, trying to break Josh's hold.

Josh lost his footing in the grass and fell, taking Burns to the ground with him. He smelled Burns's sour breath in his face.

He managed to turn Burns around so that the needle was now over the smaller man's chest. He yanked Burns backwards so that he took control not only of his arm but also of the syringe, aiming the needle directly at Burns's heart.

"Back up," he heard himself shout to the guards, who had come forward and were now standing over them. The guards obeyed, their eyes on the needle. Pat moved over beside Josh.

"Good," Josh said, getting to his feet and pulling Burns with him. "Now what?"

"Car keys," Pat said to the men, "throw them on the ground."

Burns was staring in horror at the needle just inches from his heart. When the guards hesitated to do as Pat told them, Burns said, "Give them the keys, Richie, if you don't mind."

The big man with the hangdog expression and the divot of black hair reached into his pocket and tossed the keys on the ground at Burns's feet.

"Now move over there," Pat instructed them, pointing to the edge of the clearing. "Go on!" They inched back, shuffling their feet, obviously hating to have been put in this position. The second man, with the dark complexion and protruding teeth, didn't move as quickly as his pal and instead stayed more or less defiantly where he was, blocking their way.

"Steven," Burns said to him in a pathetically quiet voice, "would you please do as she asks?" Steven eased back, but Josh knew it was only a matter of time before he tried something.

Pat picked up the keys and led the way. Josh kept a firm hold on Burns, with one eye on the insubordinate Steven. Just as they backed to the edge of the clearing, and the path that led to the cars, Steven dropped his head, snorted, and came at them.

Josh turned one way and Burns turned the other. The syringe plunged deep into Burns's heart muscle. He let out an agonized cry and slumped forward. The four of them froze, waiting to see what would happen to Brad Burns, creator of this horror virus.

Nothing happened . . . for the first few moments. Josh let go of the syringe, which was sticking into Burns's chest. Then Burns must have gotten through the initial pain and realized what had happened. He took hold of the syringe and yanked it out of his chest. Holding it up he shook it, trying to determine how much of it had been pumped into him. It looked to Josh as if all of the liquid had gone into Burns.

Josh heard a car engine start up. He turned and saw Pat behind the wheel. The assistants saw her, too. In their moment of confusion Josh took off at a run for the passenger side. He reached the car ahead of Steven, who hung on to the door handle in an attempt to get Josh out.

Pat put the car into gear and pulled away, dragging Steven for a few yards until he had to let go. Josh was able to see Brad Burns, now thrashing around among the trees like a madman, clutching his chest and crying out in a voice filled with unimaginable pain.

31

MANHEIM COULD FEEL THE RUSTLE OF THOUGHT, OF MINDS being changed, positions being shifted. The Senate floor was a quagmire of media; spectators packed the gallery, and authoritative voices rumbled. The tide was turning in his favor; he sensed instinctively that this was his greatest hour.

He had been on the floor, at the microphone, for over an hour, and he had them fired up. Normally, his colleagues would merely have been pretending to be awake for the cameras, having instructed an aide to nudge them in the event their name came up or the camera swung in their direction.

Today these nearly one hundred men and women were riveted, some of them leaning forward in their seats. They were with him. He had come armed with fire and statistics: "Sixty-five percent of all cancer-related deaths could have been prevented had the FDA acted in time to allow research firms to test products found effective in other countries. Instead, FDA officers played one pharmaceutical firm against the other, playing favorites, demanding more research, holding grudges, delaying, delaying, delaying . . . while our mothers and daughters and brothers were dying in our arms."

He could spot his detractors. This morning more than half had been against him; now more than half were in his court. He saw Harry Montefusco, fierce, conservative, self-sufficient, patriarchal. Manheim would never change Harry's mind, but those whom Montefusco usually controlled were gradually slipping into the camp of the senator from Florida.

Manheim detailed the death of his mother and of his daughter, the pain they suffered because no drugs were available. "The men and women of the FDA, many of them as frustrated as we are, are crushed under the agency's bureaucratic wheels. They must also watch their loved ones perish. I am not asking that the FDA approve everything that's brought out by the drug companies. I am instead asking them to streamline their efforts. I am imploring them to allow researchers to work with fewer restrictions. Science and medicine are not mere tools fashioned to preserve the status quo. Rather, they are the spearheads of safety and change and long, healthy life. We are a nation of iconoclasts, of risk-takers, of visionaries— men and women for whom destiny walks hand in hand with freedom.

"I beg of you, remove these destructive restrictions. Ask yourselves this before you step behind the lecterns in your home states or in these chambers: Would

271

you allow someone to censor your speeches and tell you that you cannot say what is in your heart? That is what the FDA is saying to the drug companies. Don't experiment. Don't look to the future. Don't take chances. Don't exercise your freedom for the betterment of mankind . . . until we say you can. For we are God. We will determine how much time your loved ones can spend on earth. We at the FDA are the arbiters of your fate."

Manheim noticed a disturbance at the rear of the chamber, but he was so caught up in the moment that he ignored it. "Is there a man or woman in this hall who can honestly say that he or she has not at one time or another wished that certain drugs were made available to the general population? There is too much suffering in the world to deprive our friends and family, the elderly, the young, of proper health care."

There it was again, the disturbance in the back. Raised voices. Arguments. Where were the sergeants-at-arms?

"Is there one person here who can deny that people close to him have suffered from the numbing effects of federal bureaucracy?"

What in the hell was going on back there! He was losing his audience: heads were turning; people were shifting in their seats for a look; louder voices were piping in; cameras were swinging around and crews were climbing the steps to see what was happening.

"Manheim!" He heard the voice loud and clear. "Senator Manheim!"

He heard gasps and people shouting. He removed his reading glasses from the bridge of his nose and stared up through the crowd to the top of the stairs. He saw a crowd of people, men in uniform. And a face he recognized. It belonged to . . . Pat Heller!

Be calm, now, he said to himself. Stay calm. He automatically looked to the exit doors behind the lectern. It was suddenly very hot; his skin felt prickly.

"Senator Manheim. Would you explain your affiliation with DNA, Incorporated, in McLean, Virginia, and tell your esteemed colleagues about the testing there?"

The *bitch!*

He looked up at the chairman, who shrugged and banged the gavel. "Could we have some order in here? Sergeant, what's going on up there?"

"We have some people here, sir, and a . . . and a . . ."

"Well, Sergeant?" the chairman said.

Camera crews were now moving up the steps toward the rear. Manheim knew when to cut his losses, but how in the hell was he going to get out of here?

"Senator Manheim." Pat Heller appeared out of the throng, looking haggard, as if she had slept in her clothes. Following her was a man in a beige suit coat with dark stains on it—her husband, Dr. Heller, who carried a bundle wrapped in a blanket. A network cameraman aimed his lens at the bundle. Manheim heard a baby cry.

Pat Heller was halfway down the stairs now. The cameras and lights were on her. "Is it true that you have invested millions of dollars in illegal research at DNA, knowing fully that the experimentation was costing lives?"

"I have no knowledge of that," he heard himself answering her.

"Isn't it true that just yesterday morning you took me to DNA headquarters with the idea of silencing me for trying to expose your criminal activity?"

"That's preposterous. Sergeant, can't you . . ." Manheim saw the sergeant-at-arms, and the expression on his face told him that there was nothing he could do or would do. Manheim followed the sergeant's eyes to the bundle Dr. Heller was carrying.

"Isn't it true that Dr. Brad Burns, director of DNA, Inc., has been in your employ for a number of years and that you have been fully informed about the human genetic experimentation that has been going on there?"

"I have no knowledge of what has been . . ." Manheim's voice trailed off. He felt his body collapse. The sound in the room became a din; the lights faded. He stared down at his hands, gripping the lectern.

"Isn't it true that . . ."

He felt the pressure of hands on him, voices shouting in his ears. He thought he saw something familiar, but he wasn't sure. . . .

When he was able to focus his eyes, he found himself staring down at the bundle Dr. Heller carried. In the bundle was a child with red hair and green eyes, its face covered with ugly red sores.

Curt Manheim heard a cry, but he was too stunned to recognize it as his own. All he could manage was to hold his hands in front of his face trying to blot out the sight before him.

32

THEY SAT ON LAWN CHAIRS AND DRANK LEMONADE, FEET up, heads back, facing the hot Florida sun. The sky was blue and cloudless, the air damp, leaving a light sheen settling over their skin. Above them palm fronds swayed in the breeze blowing off the Gulf of Mexico.

Heaven.

They heard a whinny and watched Amy ride her pony in the exercise circle, bumping along on her western saddle—not English. Amy now wanted to be a cowgirl and not the queen of England.

A car came up the drive, kicking up dust, and screeched to a halt twenty feet away. Out of the front seat stepped the high-spirited Julie Palmer, savior and chief engineer of the offices of Josh Heller, M.D.

"Pull up a lemonade," Josh said to her. Pat reached over and poured Julie a glass.

"I came out to tell you that I can't find Jim Ellison anywhere," Julie said, puffing in the heat. "Everything's cleaned out of his house and the office. It's as if the man never was."

"That's a very good possibility," said Josh, patting the lawn chair next to him, "take a load off."

Julie sat down and looked at her boss. "You're backed up at the office, Josh. There are . . ."

He smiled at her and patted her knee. "I'm not thinking about anything until Monday."

"I never thought I'd hear you say that." Julie dropped her elbows to her knees and looked at him suspiciously. "That was some stink you two made up there in Washington. You're both famous."

"Infamous," Pat said, "especially around here. Manheim was so popular the people would have forgiven him anything. Nobody seems disturbed that DNA was killing and disfiguring children."

Julie drained her glass, and Josh refilled it for her. "You're getting a lot of calls from women who want a checkup from the new celebrity doc in town."

"Any of them named Samantha?" asked Pat. Nobody said anything to that. The police had made their inquiries and were satisfied that Josh acted in self-defense.

Julie said, "Plus you have about ten applications from young doctors to join you in the practice."

"Any of them orphans off the streets of Washington, D.C.?" said Josh.

"Huh?"

"Never mind." Josh got up and moved a lounge chair closer. "Why don't you lie back and take it easy?"

"How can I when all this has been going on?"

"Nothing's going on anymore," said Josh. "DNA is shut down. Burns is dead. Manheim is in jail. My medical school classmates have weeded out their subversive partners. And we"—he reached over and took Pat's hand—"are pregnant."

Julie did a double take. "What!"

"Yup, Amy gets a playmate next December."

"Oh," Julie said, "this is wonderful."

"Isn't it," said Pat, feeling the sunlight on her face and the breeze rolling like soft petals over her skin.

33

~~~~~~~~~

Ely, Minnesota

ICICLES HUNG OFF THE ROOF. THE WIND WHIPPED AROUND
outside sounding like sirens from hell and beating
against the sides of the building.

Inside, a dozen men stood around a sophisticated
lab, staring down into the eerie green eyes of a
newborn baby girl. She had a large head and hands but
otherwise looked normal. The single thing that differ-
entiated her from other babies was a look of fierce
intelligence, as if there were wisdom in this face that
even the men standing around her would never comprehend.

Dr. Faubus Leung stood at the head of the operating
table. "We have come a long way, gentlemen," he said
to the others, all relatively young and dedicated
looking. They, too, had the look.

One of the young gynecologists reached down and
took the child's hand in his own. "Very cold," he said.

"Not cold," said Leung, with an almost indiscernible smile. "Call it dispassionate."

Leung moved solemnly around the table. "We have here, gentlemen, the product of years of research done by Dr. Bradley Burns and his father. You are all aware of the"—Leung searched for the proper word—"recklessness of young Dr. Burns that has made it necessary to establish this research facility in secret. We can now operate without falling under the scrutiny of the public.

"We shall proceed as before. You gentlemen and others will go to your new assignments, taking with you this vision of newborn youth."

Just then the door to the inner labs opened. Dr. Jim Ellison walked in and nodded to Faubus Leung.

Beside Dr. Ellison was a tall, breathtakingly beautiful young woman with luxuriant red hair and eyes the color of jade.

EPILOGUE

THE FOLLOWING DECEMBER 20, A BEAUTIFUL BABY WAS born to Dr. and Mrs. Josh Heller of Indian Rocks Beach, Florida. An eight-pound, five-ounce boy with thick auburn hair and bright green eyes.